THE
NEW YORKER
STORIES

Morley Callaghan

Preface by
BARRY CALLAGHAN

Exile Editions

Publishers of singular
Fiction, Poetry, Drama, Non-fiction and Graphic Books
2008

Library and Archives Canada Cataloguing in Publication

Callaghan, Morley, 1903-1990
    The New Yorker stories / Morley Callaghan ; preface by Barry Callaghan.

(Exile classics ; no. 11)

ISBN 978-1-55096-110-2

    I. Title. II. Series.

PS8505.A43N49 2008   C813'.52   C2008-901958-X

Design and Composition by Digital ReproSet
Cover Artwork by Mad Dog Design Connection Inc.
Typeset in Garamond at the Moons of Jupiter Studios
Printed in Canada by Gauvin Imprimerie

The publisher would like to acknowledge the financial assistance of
The Canada Council for the Arts, and the Ontario Arts Council–which is
an agency of the Government of Ontario.

Conseil des Arts   Canada Council
du Canada   for the Arts

ONTARIO ARTS COUNCIL
CONSEIL DES ARTS DE L'ONTARIO

Published in Canada in 2008 by Exile Editions Ltd.
144483 Southgate Road 14
General Delivery
Holstein, Ontario, N0G 2A0
info@exileeditions.com
www.ExileEditions.com

Canadian Sales Distribution: U.S. Sales Distribution:
McArthur & Company   Independent Publishers Group
c/o Harper Collins   814 North Franklin Street
1995 Markham Road   Chicago, IL 60610
Toronto, ON M1B 5M8   www.ipgbook.com
toll free: 1 800 387 0117   toll free: 1 800 888 4741

THE NEW YORKER STORIES

Editor's Note

When *Morley Callaghan's Stories* appeared in 1959 the author did not indicate the date of magazine publication for any of the fifty stories. Nor did they appear in anything close to a chronological order. Other than to say that these twenty-one stories were published in *The New Yorker* between 1928 and 1938, this volume follows the author's intentions.

CONTENTS

PREFACE

It was 1928. Morley Callaghan had published a story in Ezra Pound's' little magazine, *The Exile*, and he had appeared in *transition* with James Joyce and Gertrude Stein. He'd had a story in the Paris magazine, *This Quarter*, and so had Hemingway, and Hemingway had written to the editor, saying, "Of the two I would much rather have written the story by Morley Callaghan . . . Oh Christ, I want to write so well . . . Callaghan's story is as good as *Dubliners*."

Morley's first novel, a gangster story called *Strange Fugitive*, appeared in New York and *The Times* said, "So fresh and vivid is Mr. Callaghan's style, so sharp and convincing his characterization . . . that one has the urge to place the laurel crown on his brow without more ado."

It was hard for Morley, a good-looking but paunchy guy of twenty-five from Toronto, to keep his bearings. "I hardly ever ate them," he said, "but walking up Fifth Avenue past Scribner's bookstore and seeing the window filled with *Strange Fugitive*, I thought the world was my oyster."

Then he wrote to his editor:

Dear Perkins,
　Here is something I thought you might tell me about. Do you think The New Yorker would be a good magazine for my stories? They have never printed fiction before, but are going to start with the story of mine called "The Escapade."

Morley Callaghan

Perkins wrote back:

Dear Callaghan,
As for The New Yorker I think it has a very excellent type of
circulation from your standpoint and ours . . .

Maxwell E. Perkins

Morley was entirely at ease in New York: "Ideas were alive on the street," he said. "You could hear their footsteps."

William Carlos Williams had him to his house for supper and told him that he had found the effect of *Strange Fugitive* so stark that it had kept him awake all night.

Morley went to Paris, settled in near the city prison, had supper with Joyce, drove to Chartres with Hemingway and watched F. Scott Fitzgerald stand on his head.

Then the markets crashed.

Morley wrote a long and singular story about lesbian lovers, *No Man's Meat*, and published *It's Never Over*, a "prison" novel that Fitzgerald said was "his deathhouse masterpiece."

But the oyster bars were closed and the soup kitchens were open.

People were singing "Ten Cents a Dance" and "Brother Can You Spare a Dime."

Morley decided to backpedal home to Toronto where, audaciously, he told his friends that he was going to keep his family alive by writing "quality" stories for the New York commercial magazines: *Esquire, Harper's Bazaar, The Atlantic Monthly, Redbook*, and *The New Yorker*.

"You think you're a gambler," he told me years later. "I was a real gambler. I gambled all our lives on my talent."

As he sat down to write his stories he decided that "the root of the trouble with writing was that poets and storywriters used language to evade, to skip away from the object, because they could never bear to face the thing freshly and see it freshly for what it was in itself . . . To tell the truth cleanly."

He thought truths were unobtrusive.

He was unobtrusive.

He looked like a man who thought so well of himself that he could afford to be a bit casual.

He was his style; colloquial, clean.

He'd finish two-finger-typing a story, talking it out loud to himself as he hunched over his small portable Remington, and then he would walk downtown to Bowles Lunch to meet his best friend, the sports writer Dink Carroll, and if Dink said he liked the story after Morley read it to him, then Morley would post it in a legal size envelope to New York.

"I was going good," he said. "It was the rest of the world that had gone to hell in a hack."

He was going so good he also wrote four novels: *A Broken Journey, Such Is My Beloved, More Joy in Heaven,* and *They Shall Inherit the Earth.*

He was going so good he never looked back.

"I will never be convicted of the sin of Orpheus," he said.

Then the world crashed into war.

After the war, he wrote more stories, but then he stopped. "Everything in the world is form. I got bored, tired of the form." His diffidence was disconcerting. When he put together his collected stories, he got to forty-five and then to fifty and then he just stopped because fifty seemed like a good number. Besides, he said, he was tired of mucking around in old magazines.

But in the last years of his life, after I found twenty-six stories that he'd forgotten about, stories stuffed away with old gas and telephone bills, he sat down and carefully edited his novel, *A Passion in Rome*, and tightened the slack lines in some of his stories, dropping a few *swells*, a *gee* or two, and a *Jimminy Christmas*.

One grim winter night when Wyndham Lewis was stuck in Toronto he read these stories and wrote: "These are tales full of human sympathy – a blending of all the events of life into a pattern of tolerance and of mercy . . . beautifully replete with a message of human tolerance and love. Every one, or almost all, of these discreet miniature dramas ends softly and gently. At the end of some anguish there is peace; at the end of some bitter dispute there is reconciliation. All of these creatures are dimly aware that the parts they play – for all the sound and fury into which they may be led by the malice of nature, by the demands of instinct for animal survival, or by our terrible heritage of original sin – the roles they are called upon to take are played according to some great law, within the bounds of a rational order. The plot, however tragic, is not some diabolic and meaningless phantasy . . . There is good and evil not merely good luck and bad luck. And if the stories end in a witty sally or in a comic deflation, the wit and the comic deflation are full of a robust benevolence."

A robust benevolence.

I like that. It's clean. Fresh.

Barry Callaghan
2008

Drawing of Morley by Arthur Lismer, 1931

ALL THE YEARS
OF HER LIFE

They were closing the drugstore, and Alfred Higgins, who had just taken off his white jacket, was putting on his coat getting ready to go home. The little grey-haired man, Sam Carr, who owned the drugstore, was bending down behind the cash register, and when Alfred Higgins passed him, he looked up and said softly, "Just a moment, Alfred. One moment before you go."

The soft, confident, quiet way in which Sam Carr spoke made Alfred start to button his coat nervously. He felt sure his face was white. Sam Carr usually said, "Good night," brusquely, without looking up. In the six months he had been working in the drug-store Alfred had never heard his employer speak softly like that. His heart began to beat so loud it was hard for him to get his breath. "What is it, Mr. Carr?" he asked.

"Maybe you'd be good enough to take a few things out of your pocket and leave them here before you go," Sam Carr said.

"What things? What are you talking about?"

"You've got a compact and a lipstick and at least two tubes of toothpaste in your pockets, Alfred."

"What do you mean? Do you think I'm crazy?" Alfred blustered. His face got red and he knew he looked fierce with indignation. But Sam Carr, standing by the door with his blue eyes shining brightly behind his glasses and his lips moving underneath his grey moustache, only nodded his head a few times, and then Alfred grew very frightened and he didn't know what to say. Slowly he raised his hand and dipped it into his pocket, and with his eyes never meeting Sam Carr's eyes, he took out a blue compact and two tubes of toothpaste and a lipstick, and he laid them one by one on the counter.

"Petty thieving, eh, Alfred?" Sam Carr said. "And maybe you'd be good enough to tell me how long this has been going on."

"This is the first time I ever took anything."

"So now you think you'll tell me a lie, eh? I don't know what goes on in my own store? You've been doing this pretty steady," Sam Carr said as he went over and stood behind the cash register.

Ever since Alfred had left school he had been getting into trouble wherever he worked. He lived at home with his mother and his father, who was a printer. His two older brothers were married and his sister had got married last year, and it would have been all right for his parents if Alfred had only been able to keep a job.

While Sam Carr smiled and stroked the side of his face very delicately with the tips of his fingers, Alfred began to feel a fright growing in him that had been in him every time he had got into such trouble.

"I liked you," Sam Carr was saying. "I liked you and would have trusted you." While Alfred watched, his pale eyes alert, Sam Carr drummed with his fingers on the counter. "I don't like to call a cop in point-blank," he was saying, very worried. "You're a fool, and maybe I should call your father and tell him you're a fool. Maybe I should let them know I'm going to have you locked up."

"My father's not at home. He's a printer. He works nights," Alfred said.

"Who's at home?"

"My mother, I guess."

"Then we'll see what she says." Sam Carr went to the phone and dialed the number.

Alfred was not ashamed, but there was that deep fright growing in him, and he blurted out arrogantly, like a strong, full-grown
man, "Just a minute. You don't need to draw anybody else in.
You don't need to tell her." Yet the old, childish hope was in him,
too, the longing that someone at home would come and help
him.

"Yeah, that's right, he's in trouble," Mr. Carr was saying. "Yeah,
your boy works for me. You'd better come down in a hurry." And
when he was finished Mr. Carr went over to the door and looked
out at the street and watched the people passing in the late summer
night. "I'll keep my eye out for a cop," was all he said.

Alfred knew how his mother would come rushing in with her
eyes blazing, or maybe she would be crying, and she would push
him away when he tried to talk to her, and make him feel her
dreadful contempt; yet he longed that she might come before Mr.
Carr saw the cop on the beat passing the door.

While they waited – and it seemed a long time – they did not
speak, and when at last they heard someone tapping on the closed
door, Mr. Carr, turning the latch, said crisply, "Come in, Mrs.
Higgins." He looked hard-faced and stern.

Mrs. Higgins must have been going to bed when he tele-
phoned, for her hair was tucked in loosely under her hat, and her
hand at her throat held her light coat tight across her chest so her
dress would not show. She came in, large and plump, with a little
smile on her friendly face. Most of the store lights had been turned
out and at first she did not see Alfred, who was standing in the
shadow at the end of the counter. Yet as soon as she saw him she
did not look as Alfred thought she would look: she smiled, her grey
eyes never wavered, and with a calmness and dignity that made
them forget that her clothes seemed to have been thrown on her,
she put out her hand to Mr. Carr and said politely, "I'm Mrs.
Higgins. I'm Alfred's mother."

Mr. Carr was a bit embarrassed by her lack of fear and her simplicity, and he hardly knew what to say to her, so she asked, "Is Alfred in trouble?"

"He is. He's been taking things from the store. I caught him red-handed. Little things like compacts and toothpaste and lipsticks. Stuff he can sell easily," the proprietor said.

As she listened Mrs. Higgins looked at Alfred and nodded her head sadly, and when Sam Carr had finished she said gravely, "Is it so, Alfred?"

"Yes."

"Why have you been doing it?"

"I've been spending money, I guess."

"On what?"

"Going around with the guys, I guess," Alfred said.

Mrs. Higgins put out her hand and touched Sam Carr's arm with an understanding gentleness, and speaking as though afraid of disturbing him, she said, "If you would only listen to me before doing anything." Her simple earnestness made her shy; her humility made her falter and look away, but in a moment she was smiling gravely again, and she said with a patient dignity, "What did you intend to do, Mr. Carr?"

"I was going to get a cop. That's what I ought to do."

"Yes, I suppose so. It's not for me to say, because he's my son. Yet I sometimes think a little good advice is the best thing for a boy when he's at a certain period in his life," she said.

Alfred couldn't understand his mother's quiet composure, for if they had been at home and someone had suggested that he was going to be arrested, he knew she would be in a rage and would cry out against him. Yet now she was standing there with that gentle, pleading smile on her face, saying, "I wonder if you don't think it would be better just to let him come home with me. He looks a big fellow, doesn't he? It takes some of them a long time to get any sense," and they both stared at Alfred, who shifted away, a cosmetic showcase light shining for a moment on his thin face and the tiny pimples over his cheekbone.

But even while turning away uneasily Alfred realized that Mr. Carr had become aware that his mother was really a fine woman; he knew that Sam Carr was puzzled by his mother, as if he had expected her to come in and plead with him tearfully, and instead he was being made to feel a bit ashamed by her vast tolerance. While there was only the sound of the mother's soft, assured voice in the store, Mr. Carr began to nod his head encouragingly at her. Without being alarmed, while being just large and still and simple and hopeful, she was becoming dominant there in the dimly lit store. "Of course, I don't want to be harsh," Mr. Carr was saying, "I'll tell you what I'll do. I'll just fire him and let it go at that. How's that?" and he got up and shook hands with Mrs. Higgins, bowing low to her in deep respect.

There was such warmth and gratitude in the way she said, "I'll never forget your kindness," that Mr. Carr began to feel warm and genial himself.

"Sorry we had to meet this way," he said. "But I'm glad I got in touch with you. Just wanted to do the right thing, that's all," he said.

"It's better to meet like this than never, isn't it?" she said. Suddenly they clasped hands as if they liked each other, as if they had known each other a long time. "Good night, sir," she said.

"Good night, Mrs. Higgins. I'm truly sorry," he said.

The mother and son walked along the street together, and the mother was taking a long, firm stride as she looked ahead with her stern face full of worry. Alfred was afraid to speak to her. He was afraid of the silence that was between them, so he only looked ahead too, for the excitement and relief was still strong in him; but in a little while, going along like that in silence made him terribly aware of the strength and the sternness in her; he began to wonder what she was thinking of as she stared ahead so grimly; she seemed to have forgotten that he walked beside her; so when they were passing under the Sixth Avenue elevated and the rumble of the train seemed to break the silence, he said in his old, blustering way, "Thank God it turned out like that. I certainly won't get in a jam like that again."

"Be quiet. Don't speak to me. You've disgraced me again and again," she said bitterly.

"That's the last time. That's all I'm saying."

"Have the decency to be quiet," she snapped.

They kept on their way, looking straight ahead.

When they were at home and his mother took off her coat, Alfred saw that she was really only half-dressed, and she made him feel afraid again when she said, without even looking at him, "You're a bad lot. God forgive you. It's one thing after another and always has been. Why do you stand there stupidly? Go to bed, why don't you?" When he was going, she said, "I'll make myself a cup of tea. Mind, now, not a word about tonight to your father."

While Alfred was undressing in his bedroom, he heard his mother moving around the kitchen. She filled the kettle and put it on the stove. She moved a chair. And as he listened there was no shame in him, just wonder and a kind of admiration of her strength and repose. He could still see Sam Carr nodding his head encouragingly to her; he could hear her talking simply and earnestly, and as he sat on his bed he felt a pride in her strength. "She certainly was smooth," he thought.

At last he got up and went along to the kitchen, and when he was at the door he saw his mother pouring herself a cup of tea. He watched and he didn't move. Her face, as she sat there, was a frightened, broken face utterly unlike the face of the woman who had been so assured a little while ago in the drugstore. When she reached out and lifted the kettle to pour hot water in her cup, her hand trembled and the water splashed on the stove. Leaning back in the chair, she sighed and lifted the cup to her lips, and her lips were groping loosely as if they would never reach the cup. She swallowed the hot tea and then she straightened up in relief, though her hand holding the cup still trembled. She looked very old.

It seemed to Alfred that this was the way it had been every time he had been in trouble before, that this trembling had really been in her as she hurried out half-dressed to the drugstore. He understood why she had sat alone in the kitchen the night his young sister had kept repeating doggedly that she was getting married. Now he felt all that his mother had been thinking of as they walked along the street together a little while ago. He watched his mother, and he never spoke, but at that moment his youth seemed to be over; he knew all the years of her life by the way her hand trembled as she raised the cup to her lips.

DAY BY DAY

Late afternoon sunlight tipped the end of the bench in the park where pretty young Mrs. Winslow was resting a moment before walking home. For hours she had wandered through the department stores, looking in all the shop windows, and had finally begun to feel a quiet contentment in her heart. Every afternoon when she went out, she tried to look gay, attractive, and carefree. Now, glancing idly at an old man who bobbed his head as he passed, she hoped she would never lose this contentment. Only a few slight changes in her life, she felt, would make her happy forever.

She sat absolutely still on the bench and the sunlight no longer shone directly on the park. The sun was dipping out of sight behind the office buildings. Two well-dressed young men who were crossing by the bench turned their heads so they could see her, and one whispered something to the other and she knew they had looked at her with admiration. Mrs. Winslow became so delighted with her own peace of mind that she began to long for the few small things that ought to go with it. All of a sudden she felt like saying a prayer, but then her heart became so humble in its eagerness that she could say nothing. Her silence and her wish really became more eloquent than any prayer she could make. Timidly at first, as though it were hard to get it clear, she began to ask God to make her husband content without any suspicion of her. She asked that she might never be permitted to do anything that might make John think he was losing her. If they could only go on living together as they had done two years ago, when they first got married, she would be satisfied. She was not complaining that their plans had failed, that bad fortune was always with them, or that her husband went from one job to another and the work was always less suited to him. "What is there about me that makes him feel so uneasy?" she asked. "If I say I'm going shopping he seems suspicious, and if I dress up and put on rouge it makes him jealous. I'd stay at home all the time and wouldn't mind looking dowdy if I thought it would make him happy." Then she said, in her quiet little prayer: "Just let us go on loving each other as we used to before we were married."

She leaned back on the bench, full of rich inner consolation. It was so nice to sit on the bench and close her eyes and pretend it was the time three years ago when she and John were going dancing, first driving out to a wayside inn that served a famous chicken dinner. There had been three such fine full years before they had got married; just closing her eyes, she could see the way he used to grin and wave his hand high over his head when he came to the door to see her. She sat there with her hands in her lap, having this very satisfactory dream, without noticing that it had become twilight and many people were passing. At last she looked up at the pale lights in the office buildings around the park, sighed deeply, and then, as though awakening, said: "Oh, my goodness, what time is it?" She got up and started to hurry home.

Traffic was heavy on the streets; everybody was hurrying; but for a moment she stood on the pavement, a tall, inexpensively dressed but distinguished-looking woman whose thoughts were still so pleasing to her that she was radiant. She wished she were home so she could share her happiness; then she thought: "What's got into me? John will be home waiting. I ought to be ashamed of myself." She lived only a few blocks from the corner and she had a childish hope that somehow she might get home before her husband. When she got to the apartment, she was out of breath.

As soon as she opened the door, she heard John moving in the kitchen, moving from the cupboard to the table putting down plates for the dinner that had not been prepared. He was a tall, thin young man with short-cropped, fair, curling hair, a lean boyish face, a small, fair moustache, and worried blue eyes. He was wearing a white shirt frayed at the sleeve and old grey, unpressed trousers. For the past two months, he had had a job, a temporary one he hoped, collecting installments for a publishing house, and his thin face looked tired. When his wife saw him, she suddenly felt ashamed of her sleek hair and red lips, and more ashamed of being late. "John, darling, sit down," she said, hurrying to put on an apron. "I was out shopping and I'm late. I'm awfully sorry." But she couldn't quite take the expression of warm, secret contentment off her face.

"You'd think you'd get tired being out all the time," he grumbled as he sat down and crossed his long legs. She looked so flushed and out of breath and so neat and pretty, still glowing from hurrying and from the animation of her thoughts, he frowned and said: "You were shopping, Madge?"

"Not really," she laughed. "I didn't bring anything home."

"You're dressed up every afternoon as if you'd been some place."

"There's no harm in window shopping if I don't spend anything," she said quickly.

"Remind me that you ought to have something to spend."

"I never mention it."

"But you think it. You're so patient about it. God knows, if I thought you were more contented, I might do better."

She was so surprised, she felt like crying.

"Please don't say I'm not contented, John, please don't."

But as she watched him shift his body around on the chair, and then let his hands drop between his knees, she knew he hadn't said yet what was in his mind, and what had been agitating him while he waited for her to come home. Like a sullen boy, he suddenly blurted out: "What kept you so late, Madge? Where were you?"

"I was just around the stores," she began, smiling. She paused and considered telling him how she had sat on the bench and thought about him, then she realized he would not believe her, so she added lamely: "I thought I'd walk home, but it took quite a long time." She felt her face flushing.

"Madge," he said, watching her closely, "you're lying. I know. Good God, you're lying." He jumped up, walked over to her, put his hands on her shoulders, and said: "What were you looking so excited about when you first came in? I noticed it."

"There was nothing; I was out of breath from hurrying," she said.

He began to clutch her shoulders as if desperately aware that he could not hold her, as if he felt that she belonged completely to the life they had lived before they were married. "You might as well tell me what you did, I know you've been lying," he said. "You're lying, lying." His big hand was trembling as he took hold of her wrist, and she cried out: "Don't hurt me, John. Don't."

"Admit you're lying."

"I was lying, John; but not really.'"

"I've known it all along. Why don't you get out?"

"Let go my wrist. I've always loved you, John, I was just sitting on a bench in the park. I forgot all about the time. I got thinking and I sort of prayed everything would get better for both of us, and I sat there forgetting it was late. Can't you see I'm telling the truth?"

Dazed from his anger, he began to walk up and down the room. He muttered: "Sitting around on a bench having pipe dreams. You refuse to try and get used to things. You ought to have something to keep you home. You ought to have about six children. Anyway, I'm tired of it. It's beginning to get on my nerves."

Without looking at her, as if he were ashamed, he snatched up his coat. She heard him slam the door. Rubbing her wrist, she sat down to wait for him. She felt he would return when he was tired out from walking, taking his great, long strides, and he'd be sorry he had hurt her. Tears were in her eyes as she looked around the mean little kitchen. She had such a strange feeling of guilt. White-faced and still, she tried to ask herself what it was that was slowly driving them apart day by day.

THE SNOB

It was at the book counter in the department store that John Harcourt, the student, caught a glimpse of his father. At first he could not be sure in the crowd that pushed along the aisle, but there was something about the colour of the back of the elderly man's neck, something about the faded felt hat, that he knew very well. Harcourt was standing with the girl he loved, buying a book for her. All afternoon he had been talking to her with an anxious diligence, as if there still remained in him an innocent wonder that she should be delighted to be with him. From underneath her wide-brimmed straw hat, her face, so fair and beautifully strong with its expression of cool independence, kept turning up to him and sometimes smiled at what he said. That was the way they always talked, never daring to show much full, strong feeling. Harcourt had just bought the book, and had reached into his pocket for the money with a free, ready gesture to make it appear that he was accustomed to buying books for young ladies, when the white-haired man in the faded felt hat, at the other end of the counter, turned half toward him, and Harcourt knew he was standing only a few feet away from his father.

The young man's easy words trailed away and his voice became little more than a whisper, as if he were afraid that everyone in the store might recognize it. There was rising in him a dreadful uneasiness; something very precious that he wanted to hold seemed close to destruction. His father, standing at the end of the bargain counter, was planted squarely on his two feet, turning a book over thoughtfully in his hands. Then he took out his glasses from an old, worn leather case and adjusted them on the end of his nose, looking down over them at the book. His coat was thrown open, two buttons on his vest were undone, his grey hair was too long, and in his rather shabby clothes he looked very much like a working man, a carpenter perhaps. Such a resentment rose in young Harcourt that he wanted to cry out bitterly, "Why does he dress as if he never owned a decent suit in his life? He doesn't care what the whole world thinks of him. He never did. I've told him a hundred times he ought to wear his good clothes when he goes out. Mother's told him the same thing. He just laughs. And now Grace may see him. Grace will meet him."

So young Harcourt stood still, with his head down, feeling that something very painful was impending. Once he looked anxiously at Grace, who had turned to the bargain counter. Among those people drifting aimlessly by, getting in each other's way, using their elbows, she looked tall and splendidly alone. She was so sure of herself, her relation to the people in the aisles, the clerks behind the counter, the books on the shelves, and everything around her. Still keeping his head down and moving close, he whispered uneasily, "Let's go and have a drink somewhere, Grace."

"In a minute, dear," she said.

"Let's go now."

"In just a minute, dear," she repeated absently.

"There's not a breath of air in here. Let's go now."

"What makes you so impatient?"

"There's nothing but old books on that counter."

"There may be something here I've wanted all my life," she said, smiling at him brightly and not noticing the uneasiness in his face.

Harcourt had to move slowly behind her, getting closer to his father all the time. He could feel the space that separated them narrowing. Once he looked up with a vague, sidelong glance. But his father, red-faced and happy, was still reading the book, only now there was a meditative expression on his face, as if something in the book had stirred him and he intended to stay there reading for some time.

Old Harcourt had lots of time to amuse himself, because he was on a pension after working hard all his life. He had sent John to the university and he was eager to have him distinguish himself. Every night when John came home, whether it was early or late, he used to go into his father's and mother's bedroom and turn on the light and talk to them about the interesting things that had happened to him during the day. They listened and shared this new world with him. They both sat up in their nightclothes and, while his mother asked all the questions, his father listened attentively with his head cocked on one side and a smile or a frown on his face. The memory of all this was in John now, and there was also a desperate longing and a pain within him growing harder to bear as he glanced fearfully at his father, but he thought stubbornly, "I can't introduce him. It'll be easier for everybody if he doesn't see us. I'm not ashamed. But it will be easier. It'll be more sensible. It'll only embarrass him to see Grace." By this time he knew he was ashamed, but he felt that his shame was justified, for Grace's father had the smooth, confident manner of a man who had lived all his life among people who were rich and sure of themselves. Often, when he had been in Grace's home talking politely to her mother, John had kept on thinking of the plainness of his own home and of his parents' laughing, good-natured untidiness, and he resolved that he must make Grace's people admire him.

He looked up cautiously, for they were about eight feet away from his father, but at that moment his father, too, looked up and John's glance shifted swiftly over the aisle, over the counters, seeing nothing. As his father's blue, calm eyes stared steadily over the glasses, there was an instant when their glances might have met. Neither one could have been certain, yet John, as he turned away and began to talk to Grace hurriedly, knew surely that his father had seen him. He knew it by the steady calmness in his father's blue eyes. John's shame grew, and then humiliation sickened him as he waited and did nothing.

His father turned away, going down the aisle, walking erectly in his shabby clothes, his shoulders very straight, never once looking back.

His father would walk slowly along the street, he knew, with that meditative expression deepening and becoming grave.

Young Harcourt stood beside Grace, brushing against her soft shoulder, and made faintly aware again of the delicate scent she used. There, so close beside him, she was holding within her everything he wanted to reach out for, only now he felt a sharp hostility that made him sullen and silent.

"You were right, John," she was drawling in her soft voice. "It does get unbearable in here on a hot day. Do let's go now. Have you ever noticed that department stores after a time can make you really hate people?" But she smiled when she spoke, so he might see that she really hated no one.

"You don't like people, do you?" he said sharply.

"People? What people? What do you mean?"

"I mean," he went on irritably, "you don't like the kind of people you bump into here, for example."

"Not especially. Who does? What're you talking about?"

"Anybody could see you don't," he said recklessly. "You don't like simple, honest people, the kind of people you meet all over the city." He blurted the words out as if he wanted to shake her, but he was longing to say, "You wouldn't like my family. Why couldn't I take you home to have dinner with them? You'd turn up your nose at them, because they've no pretensions. As soon as my father saw you, he knew you wouldn't want to meet him. I could tell by the way he turned."

His father was on his way home now, he knew, and that evening at dinner they would meet. His mother and sister would talk rapidly, but his father would say nothing to him, or to anyone. There would only be Harcourt's memory of the level look in the blue eyes, and the knowledge of his father's pain as he walked away.

Grace watched John's gloomy face as they walked through the store, and she knew he was nursing some private rage, and so her own resentment and exasperation kept growing, and she said crisply, "You're entitled to your moods on a hot afternoon, I suppose, but if I feel I don't like it here, then I don't like it. You wanted to go yourself. Who likes to spend very much time in a department store on a hot afternoon? I begin to hate every stupid person that bangs into me, everybody near me. What does that make me?"

"It makes you a snob."

"So I'm a snob now?" she said angrily.

"Certainly you're a snob," he said. They were at the door and going out to the street. As they walked in the sunlight, in the crowd moving slowly down the street, he was groping for words to describe the secret thoughts he had always had about her. "I've always known how you'd feel about people I like who didn't fit into your private world," he said.

"You're a very stupid person," she said. Her face was flushed now, and it was hard for her to express her indignation, so she stared straight ahead as she walked along. They had never talked in this way, and now they were both quickly eager to hurt each other. With a flow of words, she started to argue with him, then she checked herself and said calmly, "Listen, John, I imagine you're tired of my company. There's no sense in having a drink together. I think I'd better leave you right here."

"That's fine," he said. "Good afternoon."

"Good-bye."

"Good-bye."

She started to go, she had gone two paces, but he reached out desperately and held her arm, and he was frightened, and pleading. "Please don't go, Grace."

All the anger and irritation had left him; there was just a desperate anxiety in his voice as he pleaded, "Please forgive me. I've no right to talk to you like that. I don't know why I'm so rude or what's the matter. I'm ridiculous. I'm very, very ridiculous. Please, you must forgive me. Don't leave me."

He had never talked to her so brokenly, and his sincerity, the depth of his feeling, began to stir her. While she listened, feeling all the yearning in him, they seemed to have been brought closer together by opposing each other than ever before, and she began to feel almost shy. "I don't know what's the matter. I suppose we're both irritable. It must be the weather," she said. "But I'm not angry, John."

He nodded his head miserably. He longed to tell her that he was sure she would have been charming to his father, but he had never felt so wretched in his life. He held her arm as if he must hold it or what he wanted most in the world would slip away from him, yet he kept thinking, as he would ever think, of his father walking away quietly with his head never turning.

SILK STOCKINGS

Dave Monroe went into a department store to buy silk stockings as a birthday present for his landlady's daughter, Anne. Many times he hesitated as he walked the length of the hosiery counter, and he smiled shyly at the salesgirl who was trying to help him. He was a rather stout young man, dressed conservatively in a dark overcoat with a plain white scarf, but he had such a round, smiling face that he looked more boyish than he actually was. He blushed and kept on smiling as he tried to look at many pairs of stockings very critically. He wondered whether it would help if he explained to the lady that he was getting the stockings for a girl who was very dainty and stylish, as smart as any girl anyone ever saw hurrying along the street in the evening. But all he said was: "I wonder if these mesh hose would look good with a black seal jacket and a little black muff? She has so many different dresses that you can't go by them. I want something good. I don't care whether they're expensive."

At last he paid for a pair of gun-metal mesh stockings that were so fine he could squeeze them into a ball and conceal them in his hand. When he went out to the lighted streets that were crowded with people who were hurrying home, he began to scrutinize all the well-dressed women to see if one of them had on a pair of stockings as nice as those he had in his pocket for Anne. He was anxious about the way the stockings would look on her because he had been wondering for a week what he could give her that would suggest his intimate interest in her, that would indicate he didn't want to be just a friend. He hurried, wanting to get home to the boarding house before Anne did.

His house was like most of the other boarding houses in the quiet neighbourhood except that the woodwork always looked clean and freshly painted. As soon as he opened the door he bumped into Anne's mother, Mrs. Greenleaf, a steady-eyed widow who had always been motherly and patient with Dave. They spoke cheerfully, as if they liked each other. The only time Dave ever saw a harsh, stern expression on Mrs. Greenleaf's face was in the evenings at eleven-thirty when she was walking up and down in the hall waiting for Anne to come home. If Anne happened to be only a few minutes late, her mother argued with her bitterly, as if she alone understood there was a blemish in the girl's nature. The trouble was that Mrs. Greenleaf was a prude and didn't want Anne to go out with men at all, and every time Dave heard her arguing with her daughter in the hall, he thought: "What does she think the girl's doing?"

"Is Anne home yet, Mrs. Greenleaf?"

"Not yet, but she'll be here in a minute. I've got something nice to eat because it's her birthday. Goodness, it must be crisp out; you're just bursting with good health. And here I am driven to bed with my neuralgia all down the side of my face!"

"It's nippy out, but it makes you feel good. It's a shame about that neuralgia," he said. When Mrs. Greenleaf suffered from neuralgia she took many aspirins to try to sleep. As Dave went upstairs he wondered why it was that two people like Anne and her mother, who were so sympathetic in many ways, were never able to understand each other. In his own room he put the stockings carefully under his pillow and sat down on the bed to wait. But he couldn't help thinking of the stockings on Anne's legs; in his head he was making little pictures of her hurrying along the street, a slim, stylish girl with tiny feet wearing expensive fashionable hose that anyone ought to notice, especially when she passed under a street light. Then he heard Anne coming upstairs. He could imagine her running with her coat open and billowing back, her toes hardly touching the steps. She seemed to be in a great hurry, as if she wanted to get dressed before dinner so she could go out right after eating. Dave, standing at his open door, said: "Just a minute, Anne, here's something for your birthday. And Anne, would you ever go out with me some night?"

Pulling off her hat, she held it in her left hand. Her black hair was parted in the middle and pulled back tight across her ears. She dangled the silk stockings in one hand, her expression quite serious. Then her face lit up eagerly and she said: "Oh, aren't they lovely! They're just what I wanted. Would I go out with you? I certainly would!"

"They're yours. I hoped you'd like them."

"You're a dear, Dave. I'm crazy about them. I'll wear them tonight. I could kiss you." She almost seemed ready to laugh, but her eyes were soft as she looked away bashfully. Then she crimsoned, hesitated, stood up on her tiptoes, took his head in her hands and kissed him, and then ran along the hall, leaving him standing there with a wide grin on his face.

Before she went out that night she called to him: "How do you like them, Dave?" She was standing under the hall light, holding her dress up a few inches so he could see the stockings. She was wearing her seal jacket and carrying her little black muff in one hand, and she looked so smart he said: "You look like a million dollars, Anne," he said.

"Don't the stockings look great?" she said. "Bye-bye, Dave."

He would have liked to ask her where she was going, but the main thing was that wherever she went that night, she would be wearing silk stockings that were his, and for the first time, as he thought of her, he had a feeling of possession.

That night he went to the armoury to see the fights. On his way home he went into the corner store to get a package of cigarettes. When he came out he stood on the sidewalk, lighted a cigarette, and as he looked across the street he thought he recognized the girl with the little black muff who was talking to a fellow wearing one of those long, straight dark overcoats with wide padded shoulders. A small light-grey hat was pulled down over one eye. He looked like a tough guy who had made good and bought himself some sharp clothes. "What's Anne doing with a mug like that?" Dave thought. He felt like going across the street and pushing the man away. Anne and the man moved under the light by the newsstand and he could see the man's swarthy, bluish cheek. Anne was holding his arm loosely as they argued with each other. Twice she turned to leave and each time went back and said something to him. Dave didn't actually feel angry till he saw the light shining on her silk stockings, and then he remembered the way she had kissed him and he wanted to shout across the street at her and insult her. But Anne was leaving the man, who was patting her shoulder. Instead of going away himself, the man turned, bought a morning paper at the newsstand, put a cigar in his mouth, and leaned against the post.

Dave, who was following Anne along the street, let her go into the house without catching up to her. In the hall upstairs he heard Anne answering her mother, who was calling sleepily.

"Are you in for the night, Anne?"

"Yes, I'm in, Mother," Anne said.

In his room, Dave sat on the bed, rubbing his face with his hand and trying to figure out what Anne would be doing with a guy who looked like a gangster. "No wonder her mother tries to keep an eye on her!" he thought. He felt both jealous and humiliated, and his only comforting thought was that she had promised to go out with him, too. Then he heard someone moving softly outside in the hall, tiptoeing downstairs. As he pulled his door open, he saw Anne, who still had on her fur jacket, half-way downstairs. With one hand on the banister she looked up at him, blinking, scared. He walked down toward her.

"Where are you going, Anne?" he said.

"Out for a little while," she whispered, putting her finger up to her lips. "Please be quiet, or Mother will hear you."

"You're going back to that guy you left down at the corner, I know," he said stubbornly. "I didn't think you ever sneaked out this late at night."

"Only when Mother's had neuralgia and put herself to sleep."

"Anne, don't go back."

"Dave, please; I'm in a hurry."

He stared at her, shaking his head; all evening while he had been at the armoury watching the fights, he had been dreaming of the way she had kissed him. Now he felt that her delight at his birthday gift meant nothing, her kiss was just a casual incident, and that she was hurrying out, wearing the stockings he had given her as a first intimate gesture, to meet the man on the corner. She tried to push him aside. Stuttering with rage, he said: "I know all about that guy without even speaking to him." When she didn't answer, he grabbed hold of her arm and pulled her back from the door. He was so full of jealous rage he tripped her and pushed her back on the stairs and tried to hold her there with a forearm across her chest.

"You're hurting me!" she gasped.

"I'm going to pull those stockings off you," he said, pushing her back roughly. Then she started to cry, as if he had hurt her badly, and all the energy went out of him. She was sitting on the stairs with one hand on her breast as she tried to get her breath.

"You hurt me, you hurt me," she whispered, biting her lip.

"I'm so sorry, Anne."

"You've got to watch, you can't be that rough with a girl."

"I'm sorry, sorry," he said, helping her up as if she had become so fragile he hardly dared touch her.

"I know you didn't mean to hurt me, Dave," she said, wiping her eyes. "I know you like me."

"I've always liked you, Anne."

"I like you, too," she said, taking a deep breath and looking as if she might cry again.

"Why's a girl like you going out at this hour?"

"He's all right, I've been going out with him for two years. He's been good to me, he loves me. I've got so I love him."

"Is he waiting for you?"

"Yes!"

There was a sudden fear in his heart and he said haltingly: "If you want, I'll leave the latch off the door, Anne!"

"If you want, Dave," she said, looking away. "Don't tell Mother, will you."

"I won't."

She went out. He waited, then he hurried up the stairs to put on his hat and coat. Mrs. Greenleaf must have wakened, for she called: "Did I hear you talking to somebody, Dave?" He said: "I guess you heard me coming in. It's all right, Mrs. Greenleaf." He tiptoed downstairs and went out to the street.

Anne was quite a way ahead. By the time she reached the corner, he was almost up to her, but on the other side of the street. Seeing her coming, the man who was waiting, leaning against the post, tossed his paper into a refuse can, and without saying a word, took hold of her arm possessively. They went walking along the street. Dave stood watching, increasingly resentful of the man's long, straight, wide-shouldered overcoat. Then he saw the light flash on Anne's stockings. At first he felt glad to think that something of his was going with her. The couple turned a corner. Dave hurried after them, following for three blocks till he saw them turn into a brownstone rooming house. There was only one hall light in the house. Anne was standing behind the man while he bent down and fumbled with a key in the lock. As Dave stood there, clenching his fists and not knowing whether to be angry at Anne or her mother, he was desperately uneasy, for he remembered he had called out: "It's all right, Mrs. Greenleaf." Then he saw the man against the hall light holding the door open, and Anne went in, and the door was shut.

THE WHITE PONY

It was a very beautiful white pony, and as it went round and round the stage of the village theatre the two clowns would leap over its back or whistle and make it flap its ears and shake its long white mane. Tony Jarvis, like every other kid in the audience that summer afternoon, wondered if there wasn't some way he could get close to the pony after the show and slip his arm around its neck.

If he could persuade the owners to let him ride the pony down the street, or if he could just touch it or feed it a little sugar, that would be enough. After the show he went up the alley to the back of the theatre to wait for the clowns and the pony. But the alley was jammed with kids – all the summer crowd from the city as well as the village boys – and Tony couldn't get close to the back door of the theatre. The two clowns came out, their faces still coloured with bright paint; then a big red-headed man, apparently the trainer, led the pony out. It shook its head and neighed, and all the kids laughed and rushed at it.

The big redhead, in blue overalls and an old felt hat that had the brim cut off, yelled, "Out of the way, you kids! Go on, or I'll pull the pants off you!" He began to laugh. It was the wildest, craziest, rolling laugh Tony had ever heard. The man was huge. His red hair stuck out at all angles under the lopped-off hat. He had a scar on his left cheek and his nose looked broken. Whenever the kids came close he swung his arm and they ducked, but they weren't frightened – only a little more excited. As he walked along, leading the white pony, a wide grin on his face, he seemed to be just the kind of giant for the job. If the pony started to prance or was frightened by the traffic, the big man would make a clucking noise and the pony would swing its head over to him and lick his hand with its rough tongue.

Tony followed the troupe along the street to the old garage they were using as a stable. Then the redhead yelled, "All right, beat it, kids!" and led the pony inside and closed the door. The kids stood around the closed door, wondering if accidentally it mightn't swing open. It was then that Tony left the gang and sneaked to the back of the garage. When he saw an old porch there, his heart pounded. He climbed up to the roof and crawled across the rotting shingles to the edge of a big window. At first he could see nothing. Then, with his eyes accustomed to the inner darkness, he saw the two clowns. Squatting in front of mirrors propped up on old boxes, they were scraping the paint off their faces. With a pail in his hand and singing at the top of his voice, the redhead walked over to a corner of the garage. Tony could see the pony's tail swishing back and forth.

He couldn't see the pony, but he knew it was rubbing its nose in the redhead's hand. The clowns finished cleaning their faces. One of them took a bottle out of a coat that was hanging on the wall and the redhead joined them and they all had a drink. Then the redhead began to talk. Tony couldn't make out the words, but he heard the rich rumble of the voice and saw the wide and eloquent gestures. The clowns were listening intently and grinning. Day after day he must have talked to them like that and it must have been just as wonderful every time. The white pony's tail kept swishing, and Tony could hear the pawing of the pony's hoofs on the floor.

But it was getting dark and Tony had to get home. When he tried to move, he found his legs were asleep. Pins and needles seemed to shoot through his arms. Afraid of falling, he grabbed at the window ledge and his head bumped against the pane. Before he could dodge away, the red-headed giant came over and stared up at him. "Get down out of there!" he yelled. "Get down or I'll cut your gizzard out!"

They were looking right at each other, and then Tony slid slowly off the roof. As he limped homeward, he felt an intimation of perfect happiness. He kept seeing the swishing white tail.

The next afternoon he went to the theatre with two lumps of sugar in his pocket. At the end of the show, he pushed his way through the crowd of kids and got right up by the door. When the clowns came out, most of the kids started to yell and there was pushing and shoving, but Tony hung back, keeping well over to one side of the door, ready to thrust the sugar at the pony's mouth before the redhead could stop him.

The big man appeared at the door, the pony clopping behind. In his hands the redhead was carrying two water pails, and the rein that held the pony was in his right hand also. This time, instead of going on down the alley and forcing a path through the kids, he stood still and looked around. Then he grinned at Tony. "Come here, kid," he said.

"What is it, Mister?"

"What's your name?"

"Tony Jarvis."

Maybe the big man remembered seeing his face at the window, Tony thought. Anyway, the big man's grin was wide and friendly. "How would you like to carry these pails for me?" he asked.

Tony grabbed the pails before any other kid could touch them. The big, freckled, crazy, blue-eyed face of the giant opened into a smile.

Tony walked down the alley, carrying the pails. The big redhead walked beside him, leading the pony and grinning in such a friendly fashion Tony felt sure he understood why the pony swung his head eagerly to the giant whenever he made the soft, clucking noise with his tongue. While Tony was going down the street, his mind was filled with how it would be in the garage, making friends with the pony. Even now he might have reached out and touched the pony if he hadn't had a pail in each hand. The pails were heavy because they were filled with water-soaked sponges, but Tony kept up with the big man all right, and he held the pail handles tight.

"I guess the pony's worth a lot of money," he said timidly.

"Uh?"

"I guess a lot of people want to ride him."

"Sure."

"I guess a lot of kids have wanted a little ride on him, too." Tony said. When the man nodded and looked straight ahead, Tony was so stirred up he dared not say anything more. It was under-stood between them now, he was sure. They would let him hang around the garage and maybe even have a ride on the pony.

When they got to the garage he waited while the redhead opened the door and gave the pony a gentle slap on the rump and sent it on ahead. Tony was so full of pride he thought he would choke as he started to follow the pony in.

"All right, son, I'll take the pails," the redhead said.

"It's all right. I can carry them."

"Give 'em to me."

"Can't I go in?' Tony asked, unbelieving.

"No kids in here," the redhead said brusquely, taking the pails.

"Gee, Mister," Tony cried. But the door had closed. Tony stood with his mouth open, sick at his stomach, still seeing the redhead's warm, magnificent smile. He couldn't understand. If the redhead was like that, why would the pony swing its head to him? Then he realized that that was the kind of thing men like him took for granted in the world he had wanted to grow into when he had glimpsed it from the garage window.

"You big red-headed bum!" he screamed at the closed door. "You dirty, double-crossing, red-headed cheat!"

AN ESCAPADE

Snow fell softly and the sidewalks were wet. Mrs. Rose Carey had on her galoshes and enjoyed the snow underfoot. She walked slowly, big flakes falling on her lamb coat and clinging to her hair, the falling snow giving her, in her warm coat, a feeling of self-indulgence. She stood on the corner of Bloor and Yonge, an impressive woman, tall, stout, good looking for forty-two, and waited for the traffic light. Few people were on this corner at half past eight, Sunday evening. A policeman, leaning against a big plate-glass window, idly watched her cross the road and look up to the clock on the fire hall and down the street to the theatre lights, where Reverend John Simpson held Sunday service. She had kept herself late, intending to enter the theatre unnoticed, and sit in a back seat, ready to leave as soon as the service was over. Bothered by her own shyness, she remembered that her husband had asked if Father Conley was speaking tonight in the Cathedral.

Under the theatre lights someone said to her: "This way, lady. Step this way, right along now."

She stopped abruptly, watching the little man with a long nose and green sweater, pacing up and down in front of the entrance, waving his hands. He saw her hesitating and came close to her. He had on a flat black hat, and walked with his toes turned out. "Step lively, lady," he muttered, wagging his head at her.

She was scared and would have turned away but a man got out of a car at the curb and smiled at her. "Don't be afraid of Dick," he said. The man had grey hair and a red face and wore a tie pin in a wide black tie. He was going into the theatre.

"Run along, Dick," he said and, turning to Mrs. Carey, he explained: "He's absolutely harmless. They call him Crazy Dick."

"Thank you very much," Mrs. Carey said.

"I hope he didn't keep you from going in," he said, taking off his hat. He had a generous smile.

"I didn't know him, that was all," she said, feeling foolish as he opened the door for her.

The minister was moving on stage and talking quietly. She knew it was the minister because she had seen his picture in the papers and recognized the Prince Albert coat and the four-in-hand tie with the collar open at the throat. She took three steps down the aisle, fearfully aware that many people were looking at her, and sat down, four rows from the back. Only once before had she been in a strange church, when a friend of her husband's had got married, and it hadn't seemed like church. She unbuttoned her coat, leaving a green and black scarf lying across her full breasts, and relaxed in the seat, getting her big body comfortable. Someone sat down beside her. The man with the grey hair and red face was sitting beside her. She was annoyed, she knew she was too aware of his closeness. The minister walked the length of the platform, his voice pleasant and soothing. She tried to follow the flow of words but was too restless. She had come in too late, that was the trouble. So she tried concentrating, closing her eyes, but thought of a trivial and amusing argument she had had with her husband. The minister was trying to describe the afterlife and some of his words seemed beautiful, but she had no intention of taking his religious notions seriously

The seat was uncomfortable, and she stretched a little, crossing her legs at the ankles. The minister had a lovely voice, but so far he'd said nothing sensational, and she felt out of place in the theatre and slightly ashamed.

The man on her right was sniffling. Puzzled, she watched him out of the corner of her eye, as he gently dabbed at his eyes with a large white handkerchief. The handkerchief was fresh and the creases firm. One plump hand held four corners, making a pad, and he was watching the minister intently.

She was anxious not to appear ill-bred, but a man, moved by the minister's words, or an old thought, was sitting beside her, crying. She did not glance at him again till she realized that his elbow was on the arm of her seat, supporting his chin, while he blinked and moved his head. He was feeling so bad she was uncomfortable, but thought that he looked gentlemanly, though feeling miserable. He was probably a nice man, and she was sorry for him.

She expected him to get up and go out. Other people were noticing him. A fat woman, in the seat ahead, craned her neck. Mrs. Carey wanted to slap her. The man put the handkerchief over his face and didn't lift his head. The minister was talking rapidly. Mrs. Carey suddenly felt absolutely alone in the theatre. Impulsively she touched the man's arm, leaning toward him, whispering: "I'm awfully sorry for you, sir."

She patted his arm a second time, and he looked at her helplessly, and went to speak, but merely shook his head and patted the back of her hand.

"I'm sorry," she repeated gently.

"Thank you very much."

"I hope it's all right now," she whispered.

He spoke quietly: "Something the minister said, it reminded me of my brother who died last week. My younger brother."

People in the row ahead were turning angrily. She became embarrassed, and leaned back in her seat, very dignified, and looked directly ahead, aware that the man was now holding her hand. Startled, she twitched, but he didn't notice. His thoughts seemed so far away. She reflected it could do no harm to let him hold her hand a moment, if it helped him.

She listened to the minister but didn't understand a word he was saying, and glanced curiously at the grey-haired man, who didn't look at her but still held her hand. He was handsome, and a feeling she had not had for years was inside her, her hand suddenly so sensitive. She closed her eyes. Then the minister stopped speaking and, knowing the congregation was ready to sing a hymn, she looked at his hand on hers, and at him. He had put away the handkerchief and now was smiling sadly. She avoided his eyes, removing her hand as she stood up to sing the hymn. Her cheeks were warm. She tried to stop thinking altogether. It was necessary to leave at once only she would have to squeeze by his knees to reach the aisle. She buttoned her coat while they were singing, ready to slip past him. She was surprised when he stepped out to the aisle, allowing her to pass, but didn't look at him. Erect, she walked slowly up the aisle, her eyes on the door. Then she heard steps and knew he was following. An usher held open the door and she smiled awkwardly. The usher smiled.

Outside, she took a few quick steps, then stood still, bewildered, expecting Crazy Dick to be on the street. She thought of the green sweater and funny flat hat. Through the doorway she saw the grey-haired man smiling at the usher and putting on his hat, the tie pin shining in the light. Tucking her chin into her high fur collar she walked rapidly down the street. It was snowing harder, driving along on a wind. When she got to a car stop she looked back and saw him standing on the sidewalk in front of the theatre doors. A streetcar was coming. She was sure he took a few steps toward her, but she got on the car. The conductor said, "Fares please," but hardly glancing at him, she shook wet snow from her coat and sat down, taking three deep breaths, while her cheeks tingled. She felt tired, and her heart was thumping.

She got off the car at Shuter Street. She didn't want to go straight home, and was determined to visit the Cathedral.

On the side street the snow was thick. Men from the rooming houses were shovelling the sidewalks, the shovels scraping on concrete. She lifted her eyes to the illuminated cross on the Cathedral spire. The congregation had come out half an hour ago, and she felt lonely walking in the dark toward the light

Inside the Cathedral she knelt down halfway up the centre aisle. She closed her eyes to pray, and remembered midnight mass in the Cathedral, the Archbishop with his mitre and staff, and the choir of boys' voices. A vestry door opened, a priest passed in the shadow beside the altar, took a book from a pew, and went out. She closed her eyes again and said many prayers, repeating her favourite ones over and over, but often she thought of her husband at home. She prayed hard so she could go home and not be bothered by anything that had happened in the theatre. She prayed for half an hour, feeling better gradually, till she hardly remembered the man in the theatre, and fairly satisfied, she got up and left the Cathedral.

ELLEN

Old Mr. Mason had always longed with a desperate earnestness that his daughter, Ellen, should be happy. She had lived alone with him since she had been a little girl. Years ago his wife, after a long time of bickering and secret bitterness over his failure to get along in business, had left him, left him to a long monotony of steady working days and evenings at home, listening to music from the gramophone or waiting for election time so that he could go to meetings. He had hoped for a bright joyousness in Ellen's life, and whenever he heard her laugh and saw how independently she walked along the street, and felt her cool reticence, he was sure she would be content. Ellen was a small girl with little hands and feet, blue eyes set far apart and a wide forehead and a face that tapered to her chin. She wore her clothes with grace and natural assurance.

Before going out in the evenings, whenever she had a new hat or dress and was sure of her beauty, she used to pretend to annoy her father, who was reading his paper, by saying coaxingly, "Please tell me that I don't look a fright. Could anybody say I looked pretty, Dad?" She would smile to herself with secret amusement while he was saying, "You're a beauty, Ellen. Bless my soul, if you're not! When I was young, I'd twist my neck if a girl like you passed by." Until she went out the front door he would wait, apparently interested only in the paper; then he would hurry to the window with his pipe in one hand and the paper under the other arm and watch her hurrying along the street with her short, rapid steps.

From the beginning she had been very much in love with Joe
Baton. Joe was handsome and good-natured – a big, broad-
shouldered young man with a fine head of untidy brown hair who
laughed often, was always at ease, and was marvellously gentle with
Ellen. This gentleness in such a big man used to make Mr. Mason
warm with joy, and sometimes when he went to bed after watching Joe and Ellen, it seemed wonderful that Ellen should have
the love of a man who had so much tenderness for her. Joe Baton
hadn't much money but he wanted to be an architect and he loved
the work, and he liked talking about the things he planned to do,
especially when he and Ellen had come into the house with the elation of two children after the evening out together. Ellen used to
listen to him with a grave wonder, and then, a little later, with
laughter in her eyes, she would try to get him to tease her father.
Joe could tell stories that would keep them all laughing till two
o'clock in the morning, especially if he had brought a bottle or two
of red wine. Three times Mr. Mason coaxed Joe to play a game of
checkers and then enjoyed giving him a bad beating; Joe was too
impulsive to be good at the game.

Mr. Mason hoped that Ellen and Joe would get married and
have a place of their own, and after a year, perhaps, he hoped they
might invite him to go and live with them. But instead of that, Joe
stopped coming to the house. "He's gone, It's over. We won't see
him again," Ellen said. Her solemn face could not conceal her fierce
resentment.

She went from day to day with a set little smile on her face,
and there was growing in her a strange gravity and stillness that
made her father, watching her, ache with disappointment. They
used to get up in the morning at the same hour and have break-
fast together before going out to work. Her face on these mornings
looked pinched and weary, as if she had not slept, and her blue eyes,
which at first had shown so easily that she was hurt, now had a dull

expression of despair. Yet she walked along the street in the old way, dressed smartly in bright colours, her body erect, and when she came home in the evenings and saw her father looking at her anxiously, she smiled and said, "Do you know, Dad, the most amusing thing happened today . . ." She would start to tell some trivial story, but in a few moments she was so grave again that she frightened him.

Mr. Mason was so upset that he hardly knew what he was doing. One night he left Ellen sitting by herself in the living room and went into his bedroom to read himself to sleep. He was standing on the carpet in his bare feet, staring at the reading-light with his evening paper under his arm. The pillows were propped up on the bed, as they were every night, and he patted them with his hand. At last he sighed, half smiled, and dragged himself into bed, his old body heavy with disappointment. The reading-light shone on his white head and on the intricate network of veins on his red neck as he lay back with his glasses in his hand. "There's no use worrying and wondering about these things," he said to himself, so he set his glasses firmly on his nose and started turning the pages of the paper. But no matter how he stared, or even rubbed his hand over his eyes, he kept having the same thought. He sat up and felt a surge of anger. The hand holding the paper began to tremble, his face got red with a sudden rush of blood, and it looked as if he were going to have one of his bursts of bad temper. He felt a hatred of Joe Baton, a resentment against all the days of the past year. "This has got to end," he thought. "Ellen's not going to worry herself and me into the grave. What's she doing sitting in that room by herself at this hour? I'll put an end to this once and for all."

He hurried, throwing his old brown dressing gown around him, feeling strong with independence. With his slippers slapping on the floor, and his white hair, ruffled by the pillow, sticking out from his head, he went striding along the hall to the living room.

The light was out, but from the door he could see Ellen sitting by the window with her elbows on the sill. First he coughed, then he walked over softly and sat down on a chair beside her. Moonlight was shining on the side of her face, and her wide forehead where her long hair was pushed back from her temples. He wanted to touch her cheek and her hair, but he was determined to speak firmly. He did not know how to begin such a conversation. He said very hesitantly, "Aren't you up late, Ellen?"

"Weren't you able to sleep, Dad?" she said.

"Yes, but I didn't want you sitting in here feeling alone."

"It isn't late, and I'm all right."

"The house seemed so quiet," he said. "I got thinking you might be feeling lonely. I got thinking of Joe Baton, too. Are you thinking he might still marry you?"

"He can't marry me. He's not here to marry me. He's gone away to Detroit." And, still without turning her head to look at him, she said, "It will get unpleasant for you, Dad. If you don't want me to stay here, I won't. Soon the neighbours will notice me and begin to talk."

He thought she must hear his heart beating with such slow heaviness that it hurt him, and he said, "I wasn't thinking anything like that."

"It doesn't take people long to notice things," she said.

"Ellen, it's all right. Don't waste yourself on such thoughts. I know you can't be happy, but try not to feel miserable," he said. His voice faltered, he thought he was going to lose control of himself. Then he said with simple dignity, "I'll look after you as long as I live, you know. Please don't feel miserable."

"I don't, Dad," she said, turning toward him. He saw the soft light on her face. Her face was so smooth and serene that he was startled. There was a contentment in it he had never seen before. The soft light gave her face a glow.

"Ellen," he whispered. "You look happy, child."

"I'm very happy," she said.

"Why are you so happy? How can you have such a feeling?"

"I feel very contented now, that's all," she said. "Tonight everything is so still on the street outside and in the dark here. I was so very happy while Joe was with me," she whispered. "It was as though I had never been alive before. It's so sweetly peaceful tonight, waiting, and feeling so much stirring within me, so lovely and still."

"What are you waiting for?" he asked.

"It seems now he'll come back again," she said.

"When, Ellen?"

"I don't know. I just feel that he will." She smiled patiently, with such a depth of certainty and peace that he dared not speak. For many minutes he sat beside her, stirred, and deep within him was a pain that seemed to be a part of all his years, but he could really feel nothing but her contentment now. Nothing that had ever happened to him seemed as important as this secret gladness Ellen was sharing with him.

He got up and said quietly, "I'll go now, Ellen. Good night."

"Good night, Dad," she said.

THEIR MOTHER'S
PURSE

Hal went around to see his mother and father, and while he was talking with them and wondering if he could ask for a loan, his sister Mary, who was dressed to go out for the evening, came into the room and said, "Can you let me have a little something tonight, Mother?"

She was borrowing money all the time now, and there was no excuse for her, because she was a stenographer. It was not the same for her as it was with their older brother, Stephen, who had three children, and could hardly live on his salary.

"If you could possibly spare it . . ." Mary was saying in her low and pleasant voice as she pulled on her gloves. Her easy smile, her assurance that she would not be refused, made Hal feel resentful. He knew that if he asked for money he would appear uneasy and a little ashamed, and his father would put down his paper and stare at him and his mother would sigh and look dreadfully worried, as though he were the worst kind of spendthrift.

Getting up to find her purse, their mother said, "I don't mind lending it to you, Mary, though I can't figure out what you do with your money."

"I don't seem to be doing anything with it I didn't use to do," Mary said.

"And I seem to do nothing these days but hand out money to the lot of you. I can't think how you'll get along when I'm dead."

"I don't know what you'd all do if it weren't for your mother's purse," their father said, but when he spoke he nodded his head at Hal, because he would rather make it appear that he was angry with Hal than risk offending Mary by speaking directly to her.

"If anybody wants money, they'll have to find my purse for me," their mother said. "Try and find it, Mary, and bring it to me."

Hal had always thought of Mary as his young sister, but the inscrutable expression he saw on her face as she moved round the room picking up newspapers and looking on chairs made him realize how much more self-reliant, how much apart from them she had grown in the last few years. He saw that she had become a handsome woman. In her tailored suit and hat, she looked almost beautiful, and he was suddenly glad she was his sister.

By this time his mother had got up and was trying to remember where she had put the purse when she'd come in from the store. In the way of a big woman, she moved around slowly, with a far-away expression in her eyes. The purse was large, black and flat leather, but there was never a time when his mother had been able to get up and know exactly where her purse was, though she always pretended she was going directly to where she had placed it.

Now she was at the point where her eyes were anxious as she tried to remember. Her husband, making loud clucking noises with his tongue, took off his glasses and said solemnly, "I warn you, Mrs. McArthur, you'll lose that purse some day, and then there'll be trouble and you'll be satisfied."

She looked at him impatiently. "See if you can find my purse, will you, son?" she begged Hal, and he got up to help, as he had done since he was a little boy.

Because he remembered that his mother sometimes put her purse under the pillow on her bed, he went to look in the bedroom. When he got to the door, which was half-closed, and looked in, he saw Mary standing in front of the dresser with her mother's purse in her hands. He saw at once that she had just taken out a bill and was slipping it into her own purse – he saw that it was several bills. He ducked back into the hall before she could catch sight of him. He felt helpless; he couldn't bear that she should see him.

Mary, coming out of the bedroom, called, "I found it. Here it is. Mother!"

"Where did you find it, darling?"

"Under your pillow."

"Ah, that's right. Now I remember," she said, and looked at her husband triumphantly, for she never failed to enjoy finding the purse just when it seemed to be lost forever.

As Mary handed the purse to her mother, she was smiling, cool, and unperturbed, yet Hal knew she had put several dollars into her own purse. It seemed terrible that she was able to smile and hide her thoughts like that when they had all been so close together for so many years.

"I never have the slightest fear that it's really lost," the mother said, beaming. Then they watched her, as they had watched her for years after she had found her purse; she was counting the little roll of bills. Her hand went up to her mouth. She looked thoughtful, she looked down into the depths of the purse again, and they waited, as if expecting her to cry out suddenly that the money was not all there. Then, sighing, she took out a bill, handed it to Mary, and it was over, and they never knew what she thought.

"Good night, Mother. Good night, Dad," Mary said.

"Good night, and don't be late. I worry when you're late!"

"So long, Hal."

"Just a minute," Hal called, and he followed Mary out to the hall. The groping, wondering expression on his mother's face as she counted her money had made him feel savage.

He grabbed Mary by the arm just as she was opening the door. "Wait a minute," he whispered.

"What's the matter, Hal? You're hurting my arm."

"Give that money back to them. I saw you take it."

"Hal, I needed it." She grew terribly ashamed and could not look at him. "I wouldn't take it if I didn't need it pretty bad," she whispered.

They could hear their father making some provoking remark, and they could hear the easy, triumphant answer of their mother. Without looking up, Mary began to cry, then she raised her head and begged in a frightened whisper, "Don't tell them, Hal. Please don't tell them."

"If you need the money, why didn't you ask them for it?"

"I've been asking for a little nearly every day."

"You only look after yourself, and you get plenty for that."

"Hal, let me keep it. Don't tell them."

Her hand tightened on his arm as she pleaded with him. Her face was now close against his, but he was so disgusted with her he tried to push her away. When she saw that he was treating her as though she were a cheap thief, she looked helpless and whispered, "I've got to do something. I've been sending money to Paul Farrell."

"Where is he?"

"He's gone to a sanitarium, and he had no money," she said.

In the moment while they stared at each other, he was thinking of the few times she had brought Paul Farrell to their place, and of the one night when her parents had found out that his lung was bad. They had made her promise not to see him any more, thinking it was a good thing to do before she went any further with him.

"You promised them you'd forget about him," he said.

"I married him before he went away," she said. "It takes a lot to look after him. I try to keep enough out of my pay every week to pay for my lunches and my board here, but I never seem to have enough left for Paul, and then I don't know what to do."

"You're crazy. He'll die on your hands," he whispered. "Or you'll have to go on keeping him."

"He'll get better," she said. "He'll be back in maybe a year."

There was such fierceness in her words, and her eyes shone with such ardour that he didn't know what to say to her. With a shy smile, she said, "Don't tell them, Hal."

"Okay," he said, and watched her open the door and go out. He went back to the living room, where his mother was saying grandly to his father, "Now you'll have to wait till next year to cry blue ruin." His father grinned and ducked his head behind his paper.

"Don't worry. There'll soon be a next time," he said.

"What did you want to say to Mary?" his mother asked.

"I just wanted to know if she was going my way, and she wasn't," Hal said.

And when Hal remembered Mary's frightened, imploring eyes, he knew he would keep his promise and say nothing to them. He was thinking how far apart he had grown from them; they knew very little about Mary, but these days he never told them anything about himself, either. Only his father and mother, they alone, were still close together.

THE SHINING
RED APPLE

It was the look of longing on the boy's face that made Joe Cosentino, dealer in fruits and vegetables, notice him. Joe was sitting on his high stool at the end of the counter where he sat every afternoon, looking out of the window at the bunches of bananas and the cauliflowers and the tomatoes and apples piled on the street stand, and he was watching to see that the kids on the way home from school didn't touch any of the fruit.

A skinny little boy, who was wearing a red sweater and blue overalls, stood near the end of the fruit stand by a pyramid of big red apples. With his hands linked loosely together in front of him, and his head, with the straight, untidy brown hair that hung almost down to his blue eyes, cocked over to one side, he stood looking with longing at the apples. If he moved a little to the right, he would be out of sight of the window, but even so, if he reached his hand out to take an apple, Joe, sitting at the end of the counter and watching, would surely see the hand. The sleeves of Joe's khaki shirt were rolled up, and as he sat on his stool he folded his hairy forearms across his deep chest. There wasn't much business, there seemed to be a little less every day, and sitting there week after week, he grew a little fatter and a little slower and much more meditative. The store was untidy, and the fruit and the vegetables no longer had the cool, fresh appearance they had in the stores of merchants who were prosperous.

If the kid, standing outside, had been a big, resolute-looking boy, Joe would have been alert and suspicious, but as it was, it was amusing to sit there and pretend he could feel the kid's longing for the apple growing stronger. As though making the first move in a game, Joe leaned forward suddenly, and the boy, lowering his head, shuffled a few feet away. Then Joe, whistling thinly, as if he hadn't noticed anything, got up and went out, took his handkerchief and started to polish a few of the apples on the pile. They were big, juicy-looking apples, a little over-ripe and going soft. He polished them till they gleamed and glistened in the sun. Then he said to the kid, "Fine day, eh, son?"

"Yeah," the kid said timidly.

"You live around here?"

"No."

"New around here?" Joe said.

The kid, nodding his head shyly, didn't offer to tell where he lived, so Joe, chuckling to himself, and feeling powerful because he knew so surely just what would happen, went back to the store and sat down on the stool.

At first the little kid, holding his hands behind his back, shuffled out of sight, but Joe knew he would go no farther than the end of the stand; he knew the kid would be there looking up and down the street furtively, stretching his hand out a little, then withdrawing it in fear before he touched an apple, and always staring, wanting the apple more and more.

Joe got up and yawned lazily, wetting his lips and rubbing his hand across them, and then he deliberately turned his back to the window. But at the moment when he was sure the kid would make up his mind and shoot out his hand, he swung around, and he was delighted to see how the child's hand, empty and faltering, was pulled back. "Ah, it goes just like a clock, I know just what he'll do," Joe thought. "He wants it, but he doesn't know how to take it because he's scared. Soon he wants it so much he'll have to take it. Then I catch him. That's the way it goes," and he grinned.

In a little while, doing a thing he hardly ever did, Joe went out onto the sidewalk and, paying no attention to the kid, who had jumped away nervously, he mopped his shining forehead and wiped his mouth and picked up one of the apples from the top of the pile. He munched it slowly with great relish, spitting out bits of red skin, and gnawing it down to the core. The kid's mouth dropped open, his blue eyes guileless.

After tossing the core in a wide arc far out on the street, where it lay in the sunlight and was attacked by two big flies, Joe started back into the store thinking, "Now for sure he'll grab one. He won't wait. He can't." Yet to tantalize him, he didn't go right into the store; he turned at the door, looked up at the sky, as though expecting it to rain suddenly.

While Joe was grinning and feeling pleased with his cunning, his wife came from the room at the back of the store. She was a black-haired woman, wide-hipped and slow moving, with tired brown eyes. When she stood beside her husband with her hands on her hips, she looked determined and sensible. "The baby's sleeping, I think, Joe. It's been pretty bad the way she's been going on."

"That's good," Joe said.

"She feels a lot better today."

"She's all right."

"I feel pretty tired. I think I'll lie down," she said, but she walked over to the window and looked out at the street.

Then she said sharply, "There's a kid out there near the apples. One's gone from the top."

"I sold it," Joe lied.

"Watch the kid," she said.

"O.K.," Joe said, and she went back to the bedroom.

He looked again for the kid, who stood rooted there in spite of the hostile glance of the woman. "I guess he doesn't know how to do it," Joe thought. Yet the look of helpless longing was becoming so strong in the kid's face, so bold and unashamed, that it bothered Joe and made him irritable. "Look at the face on you. Look out, kid, you'll start to cry in a minute," he said to himself. "So you think you can have everything you want, do you?" The agony of wanting was so plain in the boy's face that Joe was indignant.

In the room behind the store there was a faint whimpering and the sound of a baby stirring. "Look," Joe said to himself, as though lecturing the kid. "It's a nice baby, but it's not a boy. See what I mean? You go around with that look on your face when you want things and can't get them, people'll only laugh at you." Joe grew restless and unhappy, and he looked helplessly around the untidy store, as if looking upon his own fate.

The kid on the sidewalk, who had shuffled away till he was out of sight came edging back slowly. And Joe, getting excited, whispered, "Why doesn't he take it when he wants it so much? I couldn't catch him if he took it and ran," and he got up to be near the corner of the window, where he could see the boy's hand if it came reaching out. "Now. Right now," he whispered, really hoping it would happen.

Then he thought, "What's up with him?" for the kid was brushing by the fruit stand, one of his hands swinging loose at his side. Joe was sure the swinging hand was to knock an apple off the pile and send it rolling along the sidewalk, and he got up eagerly and leaned forward with his head close to the window.

The kid, looking up warily, saw Joe's face and grew frightened. Ducking, he ran.

"Hey!" Joe yelled, out on the sidewalk.

The kid looked around but kept on running, his legs in blue overalls pumping up and down.

Grabbing an apple and yelling, "Hey, hey, kid, you can have it!" Joe followed a few steps, but the kid wouldn't look back.

Joe stood on the sidewalk, an awful eagerness growing in him as he stared at the shining red apple, and wondered what would happen to the kid he was sure he would never see again.

ONE SPRING
NIGHT

They had been to an eleven-o'clock movie. Afterward, as they sat very late in the restaurant, Sheila was listening to Bob Davis, showing by the quiet gladness that kept coming into her face the enjoyment she felt in being with him. She was the young sister of his friend, Jack Staples. Every time Bob had been at their apartment, she had come into the room, they had laughed and joked with her, they had teased her about the way she wore her clothes, and she had always smiled and answered them in a slow, measured way.

Bob took her out a few times when he felt like having a girl to talk to who knew him and liked him. And tonight he was leaning back good-humouredly, telling her one thing and then another with the wise self-assurance he usually had when with her; but gradually, as he watched her, he found himself talking more slowly, his voice grew serious and much softer, and then finally he leaned across the table toward her as though he had just discovered that her neck was full and soft with her spring coat thrown open, and that her face under her little black straw hat tilted back on her head had a new, eager beauty. Her warm, smiling softness was so close to him that he smiled a bit shyly.

"What are you looking at, Bob?" she said.

"What is there about you that seems different tonight?" he said, and they both began to laugh lightly, as if sharing the same secret.

When they were outside, walking along arm in arm and liking the new spring night air, Sheila said quickly, "It's awfully nice out tonight. Let's keep walking a while, Bob," and she held his arm as though very sure of him.

"All right," he said. "We'll walk till we get so tired we'll have to sit on the curb. It's nearly two o'clock, but it doesn't seem to matter much, does it?"

Every step he took with Sheila leaning on his arm in this new way, and with him feeling now that she was a woman he hardly knew, made the excitement grow in him, and yet he was uneasy. He was much taller than Sheila and he kept looking down at her, and she always smiled back with frank gladness. Then he couldn't help squeezing her arm tight, and he started to talk recklessly about anything that came into his head, swinging his free arm and putting passionate eloquence into the simplest words. She was listening as she used to listen when he talked with her brother and father in the evenings, only now she wanted him to see how much she liked having him tonight all for herself. Almost pleading, she said, "Are you having a good time, Bob? Don't you like the streets at night, when there's hardly anybody on them?"

They stopped and looked along the wide avenue and up the towering, slanting faces of the buildings to the patches of night sky. Holding out her small, gloved hand in his palm, he patted it with his other hand, and they both laughed as though he had done something foolish but charming. The whole city was quieter now, the streets flowed away from them without direction, but there was always the hum underneath the silence like something restless and stirring and really touching them, as the soft, spring night air of the streets touched them, and at a store door he pulled her into the shadow and kissed her warmly, and when she didn't resist he kept on kissing her. Then they walked on again happily. He didn't care what he talked about; he talked about the advertising agency where he had gone to work the year before, and what he planned to do when he got more money, and each word had a feeling of reckless elation behind it.

For a long time they walked on aimlessly like this before he noticed that she was limping. Her face kept on turning up to him, and she laughed often, but she was really limping badly. "What's the matter, Sheila? What's the matter with your foot?" he said.

"It's my heel," she said, lifting her foot off the ground. "My shoe has been rubbing against it." She tried to laugh. "It's all right, Bob," she said, and she tried to walk on without limping.

"You can't walk like that, Sheila."

"Maybe if we just took it off for a minute, Bob, it would be all right," she said as though asking a favour of him.

"I'll take it off for you," he said, and he knelt down on one knee while she lifted her foot and balanced herself with her arm on his shoulder. He drew off the shoe gently.

"Oh, the air feels so nice and cool on my heel," she said. No one was coming along the street. For a long time he remained kneeling, caressing her ankle gently and looking up with his face full of concern. "Try and put it on now, Bob," she said. But when he pushed the shoe over the heel, she said, "Good heavens, it seems tighter than ever." She limped along for a few steps. "Maybe we should never have taken it off. There's a blister there," she said.

"It was crazy to keep on walking like this," he said. "I'll call a taxi as soon as one comes along." They were standing by the curb, with her leaning heavily on his arm, and he was feeling protective and considerate, for with her heel hurting her, she seemed more like the young girl he had known. "Look how late it is. It's nearly four o'clock," he said. "Your father will be wild."

"It's terribly late," she said.

"It's my fault. I'll tell him it was all my fault."

For a while she didn't raise her head. When she did look up at him, he thought she was frightened. "What will they say when I go home at this hour, Bob?"

"It'll be all right. I'll go right in with you," he said.

"Wouldn't it be better . . . Don't you think it would be all right if I stayed the night with Alice – with my girlfriend?"

She was so hesitant that it worried him, and he said emphatically, "It's nearly morning now, and anyway, your father knows you're with me."

"Where'll we say we've been till this hour, Bob?"

"Just walking."

"Maybe he won't believe it. Maybe he's sure by this time I'm staying with Alice. If there was some place I could go . . ." While she waited for him to answer, all that had been growing in her for such a long time was showing in the softness of her dark, sure eyes.

A half-ashamed feeling came over him and he began thinking of himself at the apartment, talking with Jack and the old man, and with Sheila coming in and listening with her face full of seriousness. "Why should you think there'll be trouble?" he said. "Your father will probably be in bed."

"I guess he will," she said quickly. "I'm silly. I ought to know that. There was nothing . . . I must have sounded silly." She began to fumble for words, and then her confusion was so deep that she could not speak.

"I'm surprised you don't know your father better than that," he said rapidly, as though offended. He was anxious to make it an argument between them over her father. He wanted to believe this himself, so he tried to think only of the nights when her father, with his white head and moustache, had talked in his good-humoured way about the old days and the old eating-places, but every one of these conversations, every one of these nights that came into his thoughts, had Sheila there, too, listening and watching. Then it got so that he could remember nothing of those times but her intense young face, which kept rising before him, although he had never been aware that he had paid much attention to her. So he said desperately, "There's the friendliest feeling in the world between your people and me. Leave it to me. We'll go back to the corner, where we can see a taxi."

They began to walk slowly to the corner, with her still limping though he held her arm firmly. He began to talk with a soft persuasiveness, eager to have her respond readily, but she only said, "I don't know what's the matter. I feel tired or something." When they were standing on the street corner, she began to cry a little.

"Poor little Sheila," he said. Then she said angrily, "Why 'poor little Sheila?' There's nothing the matter with me. I'm just tired." And they both kept looking up and down the street for a taxi.

Then one came, they got in, and he sat with his arm along the back of the seat, just touching her shoulder. He dared not tighten his arm around her, though never before had he wanted so much to be gentle with anyone; but with the street lights sometimes flashing on her face and showing the bewildered whiteness that was in it, he was scared to disturb her.

As soon as they opened the apartment door and lit the lights in the living room, they heard her father come shuffling from his bedroom. His white moustache was working up and down furiously as he kept wetting his lips, and his hair, which was always combed nicely, was mussed over his head because he had been lying down. "Where have you been till this hour, Sheila?" he said. "I kept getting up all the time. Where have you been?"

"Just walking with Bob," she said. "I'm dead tired, Dad. We lost all track of time." She spoke very calmly and then she smiled, and Bob saw how well she knew that her father loved her. Her father's face was full of concern while he peered at her, and she only smiled openly, showing no worry and saying, "Poor Daddy, I never dreamed you'd get up. I hope Jack is still sleeping."

"Jack said if you were with Bob, you were all right," Mr. Staples said. Glancing at Bob, he added curtly, "She's only eighteen, you know. I thought you had more sense."

"I guess we were fools to walk for hours like that, Mr. Staples," Bob said. "Sheila's got a big blister on her foot." Bob shook his head as if he couldn't understand why he had been so stupid.

Mr. Staples looked a long time at Sheila, and then he looked shrewdly at Bob; they were both tired and worried, and they were standing close together. Mr. Staples cleared his throat two or three times and said, "What on earth got into the pair of you?" Then he grinned suddenly and said, "Isn't it extraordinary what young people do? I'm so wide-awake now I can't sleep, I was making myself a cup of coffee. Won't you both sit down and have a cup with me? Bob?"

"I'd love to," Bob said heartily.

"You go ahead. I won't have any coffee. It would keep me awake," Sheila said.

"The water's just getting hot," Mr. Staples said. "It will be ready in a minute." Still chuckling and shaking his head, for he was glad Sheila had come in, he said, "I kept telling myself she was all right if she was with you, Bob." Bob and Mr. Staples grinned broadly at each other. But when her father spoke like this, Sheila raised her head, and Bob thought that he saw her smile at him. He wanted to smile, too, but he couldn't look at her and had to turn away uneasily. And when he did turn to her again, it was almost pleadingly, for he was thinking, "I did the only thing there was to do. It was the right thing, so why should I feel ashamed now?" and yet he kept on remembering how she had cried a little on the street corner. He longed to think of something to say that might make her smile agreeably – some gentle, simple, friendly remark that would make her feel close to him – but he could only go on remembering how yielding she had been.

Her father was saying cheerfully, "I'll go and get the coffee now."

"I don't think I'd better stay," Bob said.

"It'll only take a few minutes, " Mr. Staples said.

"I don't think I'll wait," Bob said, but Mr, Staples, smiling and shaking his head, went into the kitchen to get the coffee. Bob kept watching Sheila, who was supporting her head with her hand and frowning a little. There was some of the peacefulness in her face now that had been there days ago, only there was also a new, full softness; she was very quiet, maybe feeling again the way he had kissed her, and then she frowned as though puzzled, as though she was listening and overhearing herself say timidly, "If there was some place I could go . . ."

Growing more and more uneasy, Bob said, "It turned out all right, don't you see, Sheila?"

"What?" she said.

"There was no trouble about coming home," he said.

As she watched him without speaking, she was not at all like a young girl. Her eyes were shining. All the feeling of the whole night was surging through her; she could hardly hold all the mixed-up feeling that was stirring her, and then her face grew warm with shame and she said savagely, "Why don't you go? Why do you want to sit there talking, talking, talking?"

"I don't know," he said.

"Go on. Please go. Please," she said,

"All right, I'll go," he muttered, and he got up clumsily, his face hot with humiliation.

In the cold, early-morning light, with heavy trucks rumbling on the street, he felt tense and nervous. He could hardly remember anything that had happened. He wanted to reach out and hold that swift, ardent, yielding joy that had been so close to him. For a while he could not think at all. And then he felt a slow unfolding coming in him again, making him quick with wonder.

TIMOTHY HARSHAW'S
FLUTE

Although both were out of work, Timothy Harshaw and his wife were the happiest people in the Barrow Street house. Timothy was a very fair young man who never thought of wearing a suit coat with trousers to match, and yet somehow he looked carefully groomed and even distinguished.

In the evenings, Mr. Weeks, a bank teller who lived in the one-room apartment behind the Harshaw's, heard Timothy playing his silver flute. When Mr. Weeks could stand the flute-playing no longer, he rapped on the Harshaws' door and pretended he was making a social call. Mrs. Harshaw opened the door. A plain grey sweater made her look slim and attractive. She was at least thirty-two, but she was so effusive, with her short, straight black hair, her high-bridged nose and her sparkling eyes that she seemed like a young girl. Mr. Weeks was welcomed so enthusiastically by the Harshaws that he began to feel ashamed of his surliness; both bowed politely and hurried to get him something to drink. They explained that Timothy had learned to play the silver flute at the Sorbonne in Paris, where he had had a scholarship.

Louise Harshaw had never been to France but she talked about Paris as if she knew every boulevard, bistro, *bal musette*, and café, until she was ready to laugh at her own eagerness. On this night both the Harshaws seemed jubilant, as if they had suddenly settled all their important problems. Mr. Weeks couldn't help asking,

"What's making you so happy tonight, Mrs. Harshaw?" and she burst out at once, "We've just decided we'll never get anywhere in this country. We're going to go away for good and live in Paris, aren't we, Timothy?"

Mr. Weeks looked at Timothy, who was sitting cross-legged on the bed, holding his silver flute loosely in his hand. The Harshaws had cut the posts off their bed so it would look more like a couch. "That's right, Louise," Timothy said, his face brightening. "There's nothing here for us, Weeks. I ought to have seen that long ago. I'll live as a translator in Paris. The main thing, though, is to get there."

"Are you going right away?"

"Oh, no," they both said together, "we're awfully poor now."

"How are you going to do it, then?"

"We'll both get a job and work," they said.

"Then we'll save."

The Harshaws went out every morning looking for work. At noontime they met in Childs' restaurant and amused each other, mimicking the peculiar mannerisms of everyone they had encountered. They seemed to have all of the shining enthusiasm that makes every obstacle a stimulation. Timothy was the first to get a job, in the advertising and publicity department of a publishing house. The more he talked about it to Louise, the more he felt like celebrating, so he borrowed five dollars from the bank teller, who loaned it with reluctance, though he became more cheerful when Timothy, slapping him on the back, invited him to help spend the money. They went to a delicatessen store to buy some cheese. "People don't seem to understand that a gentleman ought to know his cheeses every bit as well as his wines," Timothy explained, and he bought brie, camembert, gorgonzola, munster, and gruyere. He also bought a bottle of red Italian wine. When they got home, Mr. Weeks thought Mrs. Harshaw might resent Timothy's initial extravagance, but instead she moved around getting plates and glasses as though they were about to start playing a new, delightful game. It occurred to her, too, to phone her friend, Selma Simpson, who did publicity for a small theatrical producer, so they would have more of a party.

That night the Harshaws talked a good deal about France. Timothy had been so happy at the Sorbonne. And, there were the trips you could take to places like Chartres: Louise was dying to see the cathedral.

"We'd like to make the whole darn tradition ours, personally, if you see what we mean," Timothy said, leaning forward.

"It sounds swell. Maybe I'll take a trip like that some day," Mr. Weeks said. "When are you going?"

"In the spring. Everybody goes to Paris in the spring – it's the season. Why don't you come with us?"

"I may at that," Mr. Weeks said, ashamed of himself for lying. Timothy was making forty dollars a week and they put ten in a bank that gave them a red bank book. In order that they would not sacrifice money on foolish pleasures, they decided to stay home at night and Timothy would teach Louise French. When they began the lessons, Louise learned rapidly. Timothy was full of joy, and they were both so pleased with themselves they thought their friend, Mr. Weeks, might like to take lessons, too. At first, Mr. Weeks tried seriously to speak French, but they were both so eager to help him he became self-conscious and made a joke of the whole business.

In the second week of November Timothy lost his job at the publishing house, for a reason that perplexed and angered him. As he told it to Louise, walking up and down rubbing his hand through his hair, it seemed ridiculous. He had got into an argument with his boss about theosophy and had suggested that modern Americans might be the ancient Egyptians reincarnated. The boss, slamming his fists on the desk, had begun to tell Timothy everything that was wrong with him – when he wrote advertising, he couldn't understand he was appealing to the masses; he was always making sly jokes for his own amusement; and anyway, it was obvious he couldn't adapt himself to the routine of the office. Timothy was fired. "There was something underhanded about it, Louise. We didn't seem to face each other like gentlemen at all." He kept looking anxiously at his wife.

Louise wanted to cry. Her face was white and pinched, as if once again in her life she had reached out and tried to touch something that had always eluded her. But she said earnestly, "It's all right, Timothy. You can't destroy your character for such people. I'll get a job and we'll go right on saving."

There were two difficult weeks when they hardly spent a cent for food, because Louise wouldn't draw money out of the bank. They ate canned soups and cereals, and were most hungry when they talked about the good times they would have in Europe in the spring.

Then they had an unbelievable piece of good fortune. They could hardly believe such luck: Louise's friend, Selma, quit her job to get married, and she asked Louise if she would like to take it. Louise wouldn't say anything; she kept swallowing hard till she went around to see the producer with Selma. He listened while Selma swore there wasn't a girl like Louise in the whole country; then he smiled benevolently. Louise got the job.

For a while the Harshaws were happier than they had been at any time since they were married; they had a splendid goal ahead of them – Europe, with a tradition and environment that would appeal to Timothy – and they had some money in the bank. Louise worked hard, rebuffed her sly, sentimental employer sweetly, and hurried home every night to Timothy, who cooked the dinner for her. He stood at the window waiting for her, with one of her aprons around his waist. He had taken a fancy to cooking.

Toward the end of December, the Harshaws had the calmness and deep inner contentment of people who can see ahead clearly.

They had one hundred and twenty dollars in the bank. They talked of going third-class on the boat. Whenever they talked for very long about it in the room, they became silent, almost hushed with expectancy, and then one night they put on their coats and hats and went out together to walk through the rain without talking at all. They went into a church and knelt with their heads down and prayed, and when they had finished praying, they sat there in the pew instead of going home. They sat there, very close together.

Then, Louise began to get very tired and nervous. Timothy noticed that she was sometimes short-tempered. When Selma, who often dropped in on them, came around intending to speak to him about Louise, he was so happy and confident he made Selma feel like an old chaperon who wasn't wanted, so she said: "Keep your eye on Louise, Timothy," and looked at him searchingly. Timothy smiled, thanked her for her solicitude, and became silent and very worried.

One night when Louise came home from work, she was so tired she couldn't eat. She sat looking at Timothy with a kind of helpless earnestness, and then she almost fainted. When he was rubbing her forehead and her wrists, she told him she was going to have a baby, and she watched him with a dogged eagerness, her whole manner full of apology. At last he took a deep breath, and said, "Good, good. That gives a man a sense of completion. Let's hope it's a boy, Louise." He became very gay. He played his flute for her. He explained he had bought a neat little machine for rolling his own cigarettes, and his good humour so pleased her he let herself whisper, "Wouldn't it be wonderful if we could have the baby born in France?"

She worked the rest of the winter, but in March she had to stop. The baby was born early one grey morning in May. Timothy had got a young obstetrical specialist who was willing to take the case without having Louise go to a hospital. It never occurred to Timothy that he would have to pay him. All that damp spring night the doctor and Timothy sat in the kitchen waiting. Timothy was polite, but he looked sick. With a mild graciousness, while the light overhead shone on his fair bright head, he talked about the Sorbonne, though sometimes he halted and listened for sounds from the other room. The doctor liked him and nodded his head patiently.

At five o'clock in the morning, the doctor called Timothy into the other room, and he went in and kissed his wife. For a moment he was so relieved he could only grin without even thinking of the baby. Louise, looking waxen-faced and fragile, smiled at Timothy and said, "We've got a boy, even if we're not in Paris, Timothy."

"It's splendid," he said, beaming with pride and relief and making her love him. He bent down and whispered, "Last time I was in Paris in the spring, it was cold and damp. The fall is a far better time, dear. Paris'll wait. It'll always be there for us."

Then the doctor beckoned to Timothy and they went back to the kitchen. The doctor said, "I might as well tell you, Mr. Harshaw, you'll have to give your wife your undivided attention for a while. However, I congratulate you." They shook hands very solemnly. "Remember, be cheerful. Don't let this interfere with your wife's plans. Do what you want to do."

"We were going to go to Europe. We won't be able to do that for a while."

"No. Not for a while, of course."

"Of course not. Not for months, anyway," Timothy said. Then they were both silent.

"If I can be of any assistance at all," the doctor said diffidently. Timothy, reflecting a moment, said eagerly, "By the way, tell me, do you know a good indoor tennis court? When Mrs. Harshaw gets up, I'd like her to take exercise. We don't want her to lose her shape, you know. She wouldn't want this to make any difference."

"I'll let you know if I hear of one," the doctor said, as he picked up his bag to leave.

Outside, the grey, misty morning had become a morning of fine, thin rain. On the street the doctor stopped suddenly, listening. He stood looking back at Timothy's place, hearing faint flute music.

YOUNGER BROTHER

Just after dark on Sunday evening five fellows from the neighbour-hood stood on the corner under the light opposite the cigar store. They were dressed in dark overcoats, fedoras, and white scarves, except Jimmie Stevens, the smallest, who was without a hat and the only one without an overcoat. Jimmie was eager to please the big fellows, who did not take him seriously because he was a few years younger. They rarely talked directly to him. So he wanted to show off. He got a laugh out of them, whirling and twisting out to the middle of the road, his body hunched down at the knees, his left arm held out and his right arm moving as though he were playing a violin, like a dancer he had seen on the stage. He sang hoarsely till one of the fellows, Bill Spiers, shouted, "What a voice, put the skids under him!" and he ran out in the road and tackled Jimmie around the waist, though not hard enough to make them both fall. He kept pushing Jimmie across the street.

Then somebody yelled, "Lay off the kid!" just as Jimmie's sister, Millie, passed the cigar store, going out for the evening. She was an unusually tall, slim blonde girl, graceful and stylish in her short beige-coloured jacket, who walked with a free, firm stride, fully aware that she was admired by the fellows at the corner, and at the same time faintly amused as though she knew she was far beyond them. She didn't speak to Jimmie as she passed, for she knew he was always there on a Sunday evening. He was glad she passed so jaun-tily and was proud and warm with satisfaction because his sister

had such fine clean lines to her body and was so smartly independent and utterly beyond any of the corner gang. Sometimes he felt
that the big fellows let him hang around because they had so much
admiration for his sister, who never spoke to them, though she knew
them.

"She's smart," Buck Thompson, a thin fellow, said, looking after
her. "If I get some dough one of these days, I'll take her out and give
her a chance."

"Fat chance for a little guy like you, just up to her shoulder," Bill
Spiers said.

"That so?"

"She got too much class for you, Buck."

"I dunno. I've known her since she was a kid. I saw her uptown
a few months ago with Muddy Maguire."

Muddy Maguire, a roughneck, had grown up around the corner
and had moved uptown. Jimmie started to snicker: "If my old lady
ever heard you say that she'd rip out your tongue." They all knew
Mrs. Stevens, a competent, practical woman, who had left her husband fourteen years ago and she had never let her daughter bring
one of the fellows near the house. Jimmie grinned, pleased that they
had given Buck the horse laugh for thinking he could get anywhere
with his sister.

Millie passed out of sight by the newsstand and one of the fellows started to sing a love song softly and the others tried to croon
with him, harmonizing as much as possible, wishing they had
enough money to take Millie Stevens out. For almost an hour they
talked intimately about girls, cursing each other.

It was nearly eleven o'clock when Jimmie went home. The
Stevenses lived in a house with freshly painted shutters, third from
the corner in a long row of old three-storey brick houses with high
steps. They lived on the ground floor and had the basement also.
Jimmie was whistling, a thin tuneless whistle, as he went up the

steps. A light was in the big front room, shining through the shutters, and Jimmie wondered if his mother, who had been out for the evening, had brought one of the neighbours home with her. He was going along the hall to the kitchen when he thought he heard Millie's voice, then a man's voice. He knew at once that his mother had not come home. "Millie's crazy bringing a guy home here," he thought. He went through to the kitchen, but he wanted to see who was talking to his sister, so he went back along the hall and quietly opened one of the big folding doors.

Millie was sitting on the sofa with Muddy Maguire. Her fur jacket and a bright scarf were tossed carelessly over the back of the sofa. "She must have come home the other way around the block," Jimmie thought. Maguire was stout with small eyes, his shiny black hair parted in the middle, self-reliant and domineering, his chest too big for his tight vest. As Jimmie saw him sitting there with his sister he felt his whole body become inert with disappointment. "What can Millie see in a guy like that?"

Millie, leaning toward Muddy, talked earnestly, her face pale, her eyes red as though she had been crying, and Muddy was leaning away from her, looking sour as though there was no mystery in her for him and he didn't want to be there, at all. Jimmie heard her say "Ma" and then suddenly she must have said something insulting to him, for he slapped her lightly across the face.

Jimmie expected Millie to tear Maguire's face with her nails; he couldn't imagine her taking anything from a guy like that; he wanted to yell at her. He couldn't understand it at all when she put her hand up to her cheek and began to cry weakly.

Then Millie said: "You promised, you know you promised."

"I was a fool," he said

"Then what did you come here for?"

"I don't know. "

"You were going to tell Ma."

Millie turned her head away from him and Muddy shrugged, and then slowly and clumsily let his hands fall on Millie's shoulder. "All right," he said, "I'm sorry, Millie."

Jimmie, trembling and angry, heard his mother coming up the front steps. He hurried back to the kitchen and waited. Mrs. Stevens, a short woman, almost shapeless in her heavy cloth coat, with firm thin lips and steady pale-blue eyes, said, "What's the matter, Jimmie?"

"Millie's in there with Muddy Maguire."

Her face got red. "In this house?" she said.

He followed his mother to the front room. Millie, resting her head against Maguire's chest, was crying quietly, both her arms around his neck as if he had become very precious to her.

Mrs. Stevens had never wanted her daughter to belong to any man, and now she said harshly: "Millie, what is this? What's the meaning of this?"

"We wanted to speak to you, Ma," Millie said timidly

Mrs. Stevens, a severe, rigid woman, had expected Millie to stand up and move away from Maguire when she spoke to her, and now she was startled to feel that Millie and this fellow were drawing closer together as they stared at her; the emotion that held Maguire and Millie together seemed suddenly to touch Mrs. Stevens and puzzle and weaken her. She stood there, getting ready to speak, yet all the severity and grimness in her own way of living seemed unimportant now. Gravely she realized why they were waiting for her, and why Millie wanted to talk to her. "Millie, my dear," she said, bending down to her daughter.

"We just want to have a few words with you, Mrs. Stevens," Maguire said with an awkward indifference.

"Go out and close the door, Jimmie," Mrs. Stevens said, trying to conceal her agitation.

Jimmie was disgusted with his mother. When Maguire had spoken to her so casually, so sure of his relation with Millie, Jimmie had expected his mother to scorch him with her sharp tongue, and yet, as he closed the door Jimmie heard his mother talking calmly, and only at times resentfully. He heard the mumbling and murmuring of their voices, and he could tell, by the few words he made out, that his mother would agree to let Maguire marry Millie.

He went back to the kitchen and put his elbows on the white enamelled table. "What's the matter with Ma?" he thought. "She should spin that chuckle-headed sap on his ear. What's got into her? Ma should do something."

As he sat there he remembered the jaunty aloof independence of Millie as she had passed the fellows on the corner that evening, and he realized she must have known she was going to meet Maguire. He began to think of her passing; it seemed tremendously important that she should keep on passing. The more he thought of it the more eager he was, and the more pleasure he got out of thinking of her going by, always aloof and beyond them, clean, with too much class, leaving them with nothing else to do but look after her and croon songs and wish they had enough money to take her out.

THE FAITHFUL
WIFE

Until a week before Christmas George worked in the station restaurant at the lunch counter. The weather was extraordinarily cold, then the sun shone strongly for a few days, though it was always cold again in the evenings. There were three other men working at the counter. They had a poor reputation. Women, unless they were careless and easygoing, never started a conversation with them over lunch at noontime. The girls at the station always avoided the red-capped negro porters and the countermen.

George was working there till he got enough money to go back home for a week and then start late in the year at college. He had wiry brown hair receding on his forehead and bad upper teeth, but he was very polite and open. Steve, the plump Italian with the waxed black moustache, who had charge of the restaurant, was very fond of George.

Many people passed the restaurant window on the way to the platform and the trains. The four men got to know some of them. Girls, brightly dressed, loitered in front of the open door, smiling at George, who saw them so often he knew their first names. Other girls, with a few minutes to spare before going back to work, used to walk up and down the tiled tunnel to the waiting room, loafing the time away, but they never glanced in at the countermen. It was cold outside, the streets were slippery, and it was warm in the station, that was all.

George watched one girl every day at noon hour. The others had also noticed her, and two or three times she came in for a cup of coffee, but she was so gentle, and aloofly pleasant, and so unobtrusively beyond them, they were afraid to try and amuse her with easy cheerful talk. George wished she had never seen him in the restaurant behind the counter, though he knew she had not noticed him at all. Her cheeks were usually rosy from the cold wind outside. When she went out of the door to walk up and down for a few minutes, an agreeable expression on her face, she never once looked back at the restaurant. George, pouring coffee, did not expect her to look back. She was about twenty-eight, pretty, rather shy, and dressed plainly and poorly in a thin, blue cloth coat. Then, one day she had on a fawn felt hat. She smiled politely at him when having a cup of coffee, and as long as possible he stood opposite her, cleaning the counter with a damp cloth.

The last night he worked at the station he went out at about half past eight in the evening, for he had an hour to himself, and then he would work till ten o'clock. In the morning he was going home, so he walked out of the station and down the side street to the docks, and was having only pleasant thoughts, passing the warehouses, looking out over the dark cold lake and liking the tang of the wind on his face. Christmas was only a week away. The falling snow was melting when it hit the sidewalk. He was glad he was through with the job at the restaurant.

An hour later, back at the counter, Steve said, "A dame just phoned you, George, and left her number."

"You know who she was?"

"No, you got too many girls, George. Don't you know the number?"

"Never saw it before."

He called the number and did not recognize the voice that answered. A woman was asking pleasantly if he remembered her. He said he did not. She said she had had a cup of coffee that afternoon at noontime, and added that she had worn a blue coat and a fawn-coloured felt hat, and even though she had not spoken to him, she thought he would remember her.

"Good Lord," he said.

She wanted to know if he would come and see her at ten-thirty that evening. He said he would, and hardly heard her giving the address. Steve and the others started to kid him brightly, but he was too astonished, wondering how she had found out his name, to bother with them. As they said good-bye to him and elbowed him in the ribs, urging him to celebrate on his last night in the city, Steve shook his head and pulled the ends of his moustache down into his lips.

The address the girl had given him was only eight blocks away, so he walked, holding his hands clenched in his pockets, for he was cold and uncertain. The brownstone, opposite a public school on a side street, was a large old rooming house. A light was in a window on the second storey over the door. Ringing the bell he didn't really expect anyone to answer, and was surprised when the girl opened the door.

"Good evening," he said shyly.

"Come upstairs," she said smiling and practical.

In the front room he took off his overcoat and hat and sat down, noticing, out of the corner of his eye, that she was slim and had nice fair hair and lovely eyes. But she was moving nervously. He had intended to ask at once how she'd found out his name, but forgot as soon as she sat down opposite him on a camp bed and smiled shyly. She had on a red woollen sweater, fitting tightly at the waist. Twice he shook his head, unable to get used to having her there opposite him, nervous and expectant. The trouble was she'd always seemed so aloof.

"You're not very friendly," she said awkwardly.

"Yes I am. I am."

"Why don't you come over here and sit beside me?"

He sat beside her on the camp bed, smiling stupidly. He was slow to see that she was waiting for him to put his arms around her. He kissed her eagerly and she held on to him, her heart thumping, and she kept on holding him, closing her eyes and breathing deeply every time he kissed her. He became very eager and she got up suddenly, walking up and down the room, looking at the cheap alarm clock on a bureau. The room was clean but poorly furnished.

"What's the matter?" he said.

"My girlfriend, the one I room with, she'll be home in twenty minutes."

"Come here anyway."

"Please sit down, please do," she said.

He sat down beside her. When he kissed her she did not object but her lips were dry, her shoulders were trembling and she kept watching the clock. Though she was holding his wrist so tightly her nails dug into the skin, he knew she would be glad when he had to go. He kissed her again and she drew her left hand slowly over her lips.

"You really must be out of here before Irene comes home," she said.

"But I've only kissed and hugged you and you're wonderful." He noticed the red ring mark on her finger.

"You sure you're not waiting for your husband to come home?" he said irritably.

Frowning, looking away, she said, "Why do you have to say that?"

"There's a ring mark on your finger."

"I can't help it," she said, and began to cry quietly. "I am waiting for my husband to come home. He'll be here at Christmas."

"Too bad. Can't we do something about it?"

"I love my husband. I do, I really do, and I'm faithful to him too."

"Maybe I'd better go," he said, feeling ridiculous.

"He's at a sanitarium. He got his spine hurt in the war, then he got tuberculosis. He's pretty bad. They've got to carry him around. We want to love each other every time we meet, but we can't."

"That's tough, poor kid. I suppose you've got to pay for him."

"Yes."

"You have many men?"

"I don't want any."

"They come here to see you?"

"No, no. I don't know what got into me. I liked you, and felt a little crazy."

"I'll slide along. What's your first name?"

"Lola. You'd better go now."

"Couldn't I see you again?" he said suddenly.

"No, you're going away tomorrow," she said, smiling confidently.

"So you've got it all figured out. Supposing I don't go?"

"Please, you must."

Her arms were trembling when she held his overcoat. She wanted him to go before Irene came home.

"You didn't give me much time," he said flatly.

"No. You're a lovely guy. Kiss me."

"You got that figured out too."

"Just kiss and hold me once more, George." She held on to him as if she did not expect to be embraced again for a long time, and he said, "I think I'll stay in the city a while longer."

"It's too bad. You've got to go. We can't see each other again."

In the poorly lighted hall she looked lovely, her cheeks were flushed. As he went out of the door and down the walk to the street he remembered that he hadn't asked how she had found out his name. Snow was falling lightly and there were hardly any footprints on the sidewalk. All he could think of was that he ought to go back to the restaurant and ask Steve for his job again. Steve was fond of him. But he knew he could not. "She had it all figured out," he muttered, turning up his coat collar.

THE RED HAT

It was the kind of hat Frances had wanted for months, plain and little and red with the narrow brim tacked back, which would look so smart and simple and expensive. There was really very little to it, it was so plain, but it was the kind of felt hat that would have made her feel confident of a sleek appearance. She stood on the pavement, her face pressed close against the shop window, a slender, tall, and good-looking girl wearing a reddish woollen dress clinging tightly to her body. On the way home from work, the last three evenings, she had stopped to look at the hat. And when she had got home she had told Mrs. Foley, who lived in the next apartment, how much the little hat appealed to her. In the window were many smart hats all very expensive. There was only one red felt hat, on a mannequin head with a silver face and very red lips.

Though Frances stood by the window a long time she had no intention of buying the hat, because her husband was out of work and they couldn't afford it; she was waiting for him to get a decent job so that she could buy clothes for herself. Not that she looked shabby, but the fall weather was a little cold, a sharp wind sometimes blowing gustily up the avenue, and in the twilight, on the way home from work with the wind blowing, she knew she ought to be wearing a light coat. In the early afternoon when the sun was shining brightly she looked neat and warm in her woolen dress.

Though she ought to have been on her way home Frances couldn't help standing there, thinking she might look beautiful in this hat if she went out with Eric for the evening. Since he had been so moody and discontented recently she now thought with pleasure of pleasing him by wearing something that would give her a new kind of elegance, of making him feel cheerful and proud of her and glad, after all, that they were married.

But the hat cost fifteen dollars. She had eighteen dollars in her purse, all that was left of her salary after shopping for groceries for the week. It was ridiculous for her to be there looking at the hat, which was obviously too expensive for her, so she smiled and walked away, putting both hands in the small pockets of her dress. She walked slowly, glancing at two women who were standing at the other end of the big window. One of the two women, the younger one, wearing a velvet coat trimmed with squirrel, said to the other: "Let's go in and try some of them on."

Hesitating and half turning, Frances thought it would be quite harmless and amusing if she went into the shop and tried on the red hat, just to see if it looked as good on her as it did on the mannequin head. It never occurred to her to buy the hat.

In the shop, she walked on soft, thick, grey carpet to the chair by the window, where she sat alone for a few minutes, waiting for one of the saleswomen to come to her. At one of the mirrors an elderly lady with bleached hair was fussing with many hats and talking to a deferential and patient saleswoman. Frances, looking at the big dominant woman with the bleached hair and the expensive clothes, felt embarrassed, because she thought it ought to be apparent to everyone in the shop, by the expression on her face, that she had no intention of taking a hat.

A deep-bosomed saleswoman, wearing black silk, smiled at Frances, appraising her carefully. Frances was the kind of customer who might look good in any one of the hats. At the same time, while looking at her, the saleswoman wondered why she wasn't wearing a coat, or at least carrying one, for the evenings were often chilly.

"I wanted to try on the little hat, the red one in the window," Frances said.

The saleswoman had decided by this time that Frances intended only to amuse herself by trying on hats, so when she took the hat from the window and handed it to Frances she smiled politely and watched her adjusting it on her head. Frances tried the hat and patted a strand of fair hair till it curled by the side of the brim. And then, because she was delighted to see that it was as attractive on her as it had been on the mannequin head with the silver face, she smiled happily, noticing in the mirror that her face was the shape of the mannequin face, a little long and narrow, the nose fine and firm, and she took out her lipstick and marked her lips. Looking in the glass again she felt elated and seemed to enjoy a kind of freedom. She felt elegant and a little haughty. Then she saw in the mirror the image of the deep-bosomed and polite saleslady.

"It is nice, isn't it?" Frances said, wishing suddenly that she hadn't come into the store.

"It is wonderfully becoming to you, especially to you."

And Frances said suddenly: "I suppose I could change it, if my husband didn't like it."

"Of course."

"Then I'll take it."

Even while paying for the hat and assuring herself that it would be amusing to take it home for the evening, she had a feeling that she ought to have known when she first came into the store that she intended to take the hat home. The saleswoman was smiling. Frances, no longer embarrassed, thought with pleasure of going out with Eric and wearing the hat, tucking the price tag up into her hair. In the morning she could return it.

But as she walked out of the store there was a hope way down within her that Eric would find her so charming in the red hat he would insist she keep it. She wanted him to be freshly aware of her, to like the hat, to discover its restrained elegance. And when they went out together for the evening they would both share the feeling she had had when first she had looked in the shop window. Frances, carrying the box, hurried, eager to get home. The sharp wind had gone down. When there was no wind on these fall evenings it was not cold, and she would not have to wear a coat with her woolen dress. It was just about dark now and all the lights were lit in the streets.

The stairs in the apartment house were long, and on other evenings very tiring, but tonight she seemed to be breathing lightly as she opened the door. Her husband was sitting by the table lamp, reading the paper. A black-haired man with a well-shaped nose, he seemed utterly without energy, slumped down in the chair. A slight odour of whiskey came from him. For four months he had been out of work and some of the spirit had gone out of him, as if he felt that he could never again have independence, and most of the afternoon he had been standing in the streets by the theatres, talking with actors who were out of work.

"Hello, Eric boy," she said, kissing him on the head.

"'Lo France," he said.

"Let's go out and eat tonight," she said.

"What with?"

"Bucks, big boy, a couple of dollar dinners."

He had hardly looked at her. She went into the bedroom and took the hat out of the box, adjusting it on her head to the right angle, lightly powdering her nose and smiling cheerfully. Jauntily she walked into the living room, swinging her hips a little and trying not to smile too openly.

"Take a look at the hat, Eric. How would you like to step out with me?"

Smiling faintly, he said: "You look snappy, but you can't afford a hat."

"Never mind that. How do you like it?"

"What's the use if you can't keep it."

"Did you ever see anything look so good on me?"

"Was it bargain day somewhere?"

"Bargain day! Fifteen bucks at one of the best shops!"

"You'd bother looking at fifteen-dollar hats with me out of work," he said angrily, getting up and glaring at her.

"I would."

"It's your money. You do what you want."

Frances felt hurt, as if for months there had been a steady pressure on her, and she said stubbornly: "I paid for it. Of course, I can take it back if you insist."

"If I insist," he said, getting up slowly and sneering at her as though he had been hating her for months. "*If I insist*. And you know how I feel about the whole business."

Frances felt hurt and yet strong from indignation, so shrugged her shoulders. "I wanted to wear it tonight," she said.

His face was white, his eyes almost closed. Suddenly he grabbed hold of her by the wrist, twisting it till she sank down on one knee.

"You'll get rid of that hat or I'll break every bone in your body. I'll clear out of here for good."

"Eric, please."

"You've been keeping me, haven't you?"

"Don't, Eric."

"Get your fifteen-buck hat out of my sight. Get rid of it, or I'll get out of here for good."

He snatched the hat from her head, pulling it, twisting it in his hands, then throwing it on the floor. He kicked it across the room. "Get it out of here or we're through."

The indignation had gone out of Frances. She was afraid of him; afraid, too, that he would suddenly rush out of the room and never come back, for she knew he had thought of doing it before. Picking up the hat she caressed the soft felt with her fingers, though she could hardly see it with her eyes filled with tears. The felt was creased, the price tag had been torn off, leaving a tiny tear at the back.

Eric was sitting there, watching her.

The hat was torn and she could not take it back. She put it in the box, wrapping the tissue paper around it, and then she went along the hall to Mrs. Foley's apartment.

Mrs. Foley, a smiling, fat woman with a round, cheerful face, opened the door. She saw Frances was agitated and felt sorry for her. "Frances, dear, what's the matter with you?"

"You remember the hat I was telling you about? Here it is. It doesn't look good on me. I was disappointed and pulled it off my head and there's a tiny tear in it. Maybe you'd want it."

Mrs. Foley thought at once that Frances had been quarreling with her husband. Mrs. Foley held up the hat and looked at it shrewdly. Then she went back into her bedroom and tried it on. The felt was good, and though it had been creased, it was quite smooth now. "Of course, I never pay more than five dollars for a hat," she said. The little felt hat did not look good on her round head and face.

"I hate to offer you five dollars for it, Frances, but . . ."

"All right. Give me five dollars."

As Mrs. Foley took the five dollars from her purse, Frances said suddenly: "Listen, dear, if I want it back next week you'll sell it back to me for five?"

"Sure I will, kid."

Frances hurried to her own apartment. Though she knew Eric could not have gone out while she was standing in the hall, she kept on saying to herself: "Please, Heaven, please don't let me do anything to make him leave me while he's feeling this way."

Eric, with his arms folded across his chest, was looking out of the window. Frances put the five dollars Mrs. Foley had given her, and the three dollars left over from her salary, on the small table by Eric's chair. "I sold it to Mrs. Foley," she said.

"Thanks," he said, without looking at her,

"I'm absolutely satisfied," she said, softly and sincerely.

"All right, I'm sorry," he said briefly.

"I mean I don't know what makes you think I'm not satisfied – that's all," she said.

Sitting beside him she put her elbow on her knee and thought of the felt hat on Mrs. Foley's head: it did not look good on her; her face was not the shape of the long silver face of the mannequin head. As Frances thought of the way the hat had looked on the head in the window she hoped vaguely that something would turn up so that she could get it back from Mrs. Foley by the end of the week. And just thinking of it, she felt that faint haughty elation; it was a plain little red hat, the kind of hat she had wanted for months, elegant and expensive, a plain felt hat, so very distinctive.

THE DUEL

In their light summer suits they kept coming up the steps from the Christopher Street subway into the warm night, their bright faces moving from the shadow into the street light. Sometimes they came slowly in groups, but those who were alone hurried when they reached the street. At first there were so many girls that Luther Simpson, standing a little piece away on Seventh Avenue, thought Inez would surely be among them. "She'll be on the next train," he thought. "If she's not on that, I'll only wait three trains more."

He grew more and more desolate, more uncertain and fearful, and yet, looking along the lighted avenue and remembering how often he and Inez had been among these people at this hour, he felt eager and almost hopeful. This was his neighbourhood, here among these people; they looked just the same as they did on any other night when he and Inez were together. At any moment she was apt to come hurrying along; she would try hard to look severe, smile in spite of herself, look very lovely, start to speak, and then maybe laugh a little instead, and then they would link arms awkwardly and walk in silence.

But because he could not help feeling fearful, Luther started to walk along the side street toward her house, so he would be sure of not missing her. When he was nearly there a taxi stopped a few houses away with the engine running. The driver turned and hung open the door, and there was a little movement of his shoulders as he made himself more comfortable in his seat. Then the engine was turned off. After what seemed a very long time a big man in a grey flannel suit stepped out and then helped Inez to the pavement. He helped her out with a special tenderness, and when he made a little bow to her the light shone on his high forehead and black hair. "Good night, Inez. You're a darling," he was saying.

She was smiling; her face looked more lovely than Luther had thought it would look when he was thinking of her coming along and smiling at him. "It was such a super time," she said gaily.

"Dream about it," the man said, grinning.

"I'll try hard," she called as she turned, waving her hand. Her face in that light was full of a glowing excitement; there was a reckless, laughing joy in it that Luther had never seen before, as if she had just come from some kind of delightful amusement she had not known for a long time, something that had left her a little breathless. The sound of her laughter scared Luther. It seemed to be the very sound he had been waiting for so fearfully. Now, in her white linen suit and white shoes, she was going across the pavement. She was taking the key out of her purse. Pausing an instant, she pulled off her hat and shook her thick, dark hair free. And then, as she opened the door, he called out sharply, "Inez, Inez, wait a minute."

Startled, she turned, but she did not speak. She stood there watching him coming toward her, and when he was close to her she said in a cool, even tone, "What do you want, Luther?"

"What were you doing with that guy, Inez? Where have you been?" He took hold of her by the arm as if she had always belonged to him and now he was entitled to punish her, but when she pulled her arm away so very firmly he stopped speaking, as if he could not get his breath.

"It's none of your business where I was, Luther," she said. "I'm going in now, if you don't mind."

"Who was that guy?"

"I won't tell you."

"Was that the first time you were out with him?"

"I won't tell you," she said wearily. "I'm going in."

He was trying to think of something harsh to say that would hurt her, but as he realized how aloof she was, how untouched by his presence, he grew frightened, and he said, "Listen, I was only kidding the other night. I'm not sore now, I love you, Inez. Only you should have said you were going out with someone else when I phoned. You said you were going to see your cousin."

"Supposing I did."

"Well . . . you ought . . . Never mind that. I'm not sore. I can understand you might want to see a show sometimes like we used to. Were you at a show? See, I'm not sore. Look at me." Luther was trying to smile like an amiable young man who was happy to see people having a good time, but when Inez did look up at him she wasn't reassured at all.

She grew very agitated and said angrily, "You've got a nerve, Luther. You weren't content to leave things the way they were. Any girl would get tired of the way you go . . ." She didn't finish, she felt an ache growing in her for all the good times they had had during these last three years. Every trivial pleasure they had shared seemed to have an intense meaning now. And then she blurted out, "I'm sick and tired of the way you've been going on, Luther. That's all over, I've made up my mind."

"No, you haven't, Inez. I was irritable the other night. I was thinking I'd never get work. I was thinking we'd never be able to get married. I was thinking I'd go crazy."

"Did I ever complain?"

"No. You really didn't."

"You said yourself you were fed up."

"I wasn't fed up with you, Inez. I was fed up with borrowing money from you and letting you do things for me. It got so it was terrible having you buy coffee and things like that for us, don't you see?"

"I didn't say anything, but you kept yelling at me that I was discontented."

"I meant I'd like to be able to be doing little things for you. That's why I started to quarrel and shout at you."

"You kept saying it so often now I believe it," she said, taking a deep breath and then, sighing wearily, "Maybe I *was* discontented."

"Did I really make you feel it was all hopeless?"

"Yes, you did."

"Then I'm a nut. I love you."

With her face turned away, as if she dared not listen, she started to go into the apartment house. She did not want him to see how bewildered she was. As she opened the door she said so softly that he could hardly hear, "Good night, Luther."

"I won't go. You can't do a thing like that. Tell me where you were tonight," and he pressed his face against the glass of the door, catching a last glimpse of her ankles and then her shoes as she went up the stairs. At first he was so resentful that he wanted to pound on the door with his fist, but almost at once he felt weak and spent, and he walked away and crossed the road so he could look up at her apartment.

Standing there, he waited to see her shadow pass across the lowered window shade as she moved around the room, but there was no shadow, nothing to show she was in the room. At last he noticed the faintest movement of the window drape, low down, at the corner, and then a little thin streak of light. Someone was there, peering out at the street. She was watching him, he knew, trying to hide, probably kneeling on the floor with her eyes level with the windowsill. He felt a surge of joy. Inez could not leave him like that. She had to watch him. She had to kneel there, feeling herself pulled strongly toward him, unable to go while he was looking up at her window.

But it was very hard to have her up there and not be able to talk to her. He felt now a vast apology in himself for anything he might have done to destroy the tenderness she had felt for him. It was so splendid to be able to hold her there, making her watch him, that he longed to be able to do something that would coax her back to him; and he kept growing more hopeful, as if he had only to keep looking at the window faithfully for awhile and the drape would be pulled to one side, the shade raised, and she would beckon to him. The same summer night air, the same murmur of city sounds, were there around them now as they had been on other nights, when they had felt so close to one another. If only she could hear him, how he would plead with her. He whispered, "I'm not sore, only you should have said you were going out with someone when I phoned." He knew that she was kneeling there, feeling the struggle within her; all her restlessness and the bitterness of the last few days were pulling her one way, and something much deeper, that weakened her and filled her with melancholy, was resisting strongly. He said aloud, "That guy didn't mean a thing, you just wanted a little amusement, right?"

As he kept looking up at the window, he grew full of persuasion, full of confidence because he still held her there. All the love between them that had been built up out of so many fine, hopeful, eager moments was offering too much resistance to the bitterness that was pulling her the other way.

Knowing her so close to him, he began to feel a new boldness; he felt that she must have been persuaded and had yielded to him. He began to move across the street, looking up at the lighted room.

But when he reached the middle of the street, it was as though the struggle had been decided: she had left the window he knew, for in the room the light was turned out.

Running ahead, he rang the apartment bell; he waited, and then rang again, and then kept on ringing. There was no answer, and he wanted to shout, "She thinks I'm crazy? All right. All right."

He ran to the corner, his thoughts raced with him: "She thinks she won't make a mistake. She thinks I'll never get anywhere, I can't show a girl the town, like that guy that rides in taxicabs. I'll get money, I'll get clothes, I'll get girls, pretty girls." These thoughts rushed through his mind as though he had become buoyant and confident. He reached the corner and stood looking up Seventh Avenue. There was no breeze, and the air was warm and muggy. He looked up the street as far as he could, and then he took a deep, tired breath.

ABSOLUTION

Jennie Hughes had been a steady customer at Jerry Mallory's bar. She was about forty-five years old, the wife of a lawyer who had abandoned her ten years ago, but who still sent her money to pay for her room and liquor. At one time she had been active and shapely; now she was slow and stout and her cheeks were criss-crossed with fine transparent veins. When she had first come to the neighbourhood people called her Mrs. Hughes, but now everybody called her Jennie.

When she was not quite sober, if anybody in her street dis-turbed her, she was apt to yell and scream at the top of her voice. Neighbours, who at one time had felt sorry for her, were now anx-ious to have her move away. Jennie's landlady, Mrs. Turner, had been trying for two months to get rid of her, but Mrs. Turner had been unfortunate enough to try to argue the question when Jennie was tipsy.

One night Jennie was wondering if Jerry Mallory would give her whiskey on credit. For two weeks she hadn't paid him. She had been drinking in the afternoon and now felt it necessary to have a bottle for Sunday. There were only about two fingers in the bottle standing on the bureau. She put on her hat and looked at herself in the mirror. Though she was aware that styles changed, she didn't seem able to keep up with them; now she was wearing a short skirt when everybody else was wearing their dresses long, and two years ago she had worn a long dress when other women were wearing short skirts. She heard somebody coming up the stairs. Turning, and staring at the door, for she expected her landlady to appear, she thrust her chin out angrily. "Come in," she called out when there was a knock on the door.

A man over six feet came in, a big serious-looking priest with thin grey hair, a large red face, and a tiny nose. "Good evening, Mrs. Hughes," he said politely without smiling.

"Good evening, Father," Jennie said. She had never seen the man before and she began to feel uneasy, nervous and ashamed of herself as she looked at the bottle on the bureau. She said suddenly, and shrewdly: "Did somebody send you here, father?"

"Now never mind that," the priest said. "It's enough that I'm here and you can thank God that I came." He was an old, serious, unsentimental priest who was not at all impressed by the fawning smile and the little bow she made for him. Shaking his head to show his disgust with her, he said flatly: "Mrs. Hughes, there's nothing more degrading in this world than a tipsy woman. A drunken man, Lord knows, is bad enough, but a drunken woman is somehow lower than a beast in the field."

Jennie's pride was hurt, and she said angrily, without inviting him to sit down: "Who sent you here? Who sent you here to butt into my business? Tell me that."

"Now listen to me, Mrs. Hughes. It's time someone brought you to your senses."

"You don't know me. I don't know you," Jennie said abruptly.

"I know all about you. I know you ought to be looking after your two children. But I'm not going to argue with you. I want to give you a very solemn warning. If you don't change your life you'll go straight to hell."

"You leave me alone, do you hear? Go on away," Jennie said.

"And I'll tell you this," he said, bending close to her and lifting his finger. "If you were to die at this moment and I were asked to give you absolution I doubt if my conscience would permit me to do it. Now for God's sake, woman, straighten up. Go to church. Go this night to confession and ask God to forgive you. Promise me you'll go to confession. At one time you must have been a decent Catholic woman. Promise me."

"You can't force me to do anything I don't want to do. I know. It was that Mrs. Turner that sent you here. I'll fix her. And don't you butt in either," Jennie said.

The big priest nodded his head with a kind of final and savage warning, and went out without saying another word.

As a defiant gesture Jennie drained the last inch of whiskey from the bottle and muttered: "Trying to drive me to confession, eh?" She decided to go to Jerry Mallory's bar at once.

The drink of whiskey made Jennie tipsy. The old priest had said she would go to hell when she died, and she felt like crying. With a serious expression on her face she walked along the lighted street, a stout woman in a short skirt leaning forward a bit, her wide velvet hat too far back on her head. She tried to remember the faces of her two children, a boy and a girl. The priest had aroused in her an uneasy longing for a time she was hardly able to recall, a time when she had gone to church, and gone to confession too, when she was a much younger woman.

Approaching the bar, whose drawn blinds concealed the light inside, she wondered what she might say to Mallory. The doorman, who let her in, nodded familiarly without speaking, and she went through to the lighted barroom. No one paid any attention to her. Men and women were standing at the bar, sitting at the tables by the door, or at the small tables opposite the bar. Jennie sat down by herself. She could see Jerry, clean-shaven and neat in his blue suit, smiling affably at everybody and sometimes helping the busy young man, Henry, to pass drinks across the bar.

Finally Henry, looking competent with his sleeves rolled up and his bow tie, came over to Jennie and said: "Hello, Jennie, what'll it be tonight?"

"I'd like a little gin, to take out with me," she said soothingly. "And tell Jerry I'll fix it up with him next week. How are you, Henry?" She hoped he could see how nicely she was smiling.

"I don't know, Jennie," he said doubtfully.

"Look here, you know I'll pay at the end of the month."

"It's like this," Henry said. "I'd do it. You know that. But the boss won't let me."

"Then let me speak to Jerry," she said brusquely.

In a moment Henry returned and said: "Jerry's awfully busy right now, Jennie. Maybe some other time. . ."

"I'll sit here and wait," Jennie said, folding her arms. "I'll sit right here till doomsday and wait."

"All right. But he's awfully busy. He may not come."

Jennie waited and nobody paid any attention to her. She felt tired. As she crossed her legs at the ankles and put her head back against the wall, she felt drowsy and dizzy. "I oughtn't to have taken that last drink before coming here," she thought. She tried to keep awake, muttering, "That old priest couldn't scare me," having the most disconnected thoughts about Eastertime and choir music. Soon she fell sound asleep.

She began to breathe so heavily that customers at the bar, turning, snickered. Looking over at her, Jerry Mallory frowned. She was an old, though difficult, customer, so he went over to her and shook her shoulder lightly. She stirred, waking. It had been very strong in her thoughts that the old priest had wanted her to go to confession and now, only half-awake, she mumbled uneasily: "Bless me, father, for I have sinned."

"Hey, Jennie, where do you think you are? Bless you, old girl," he said, starting to laugh.

"Oh, it's you, Jerry. I forgot where I was."

She was wide awake, so sober he thought she might have been deliberately kidding him. He laughed loudly. "You're a card, Jennie!" he said. "You're a grand old gal. And I'll get you a little gin for old times' sake."

He turned and said to the three men at the bar who were nearest to him: "Did you hear what Jennie just pulled on me?"

Jennie was ashamed. She stood up, in her skirt that was too short, with her black velvet hat too far back on her head. The men started to laugh. Then they started to laugh louder and louder. The sound of their laughter at first made Jennie angry, with something of a fine woman's disgust, and then, with humility, she felt herself reaching out toward a faintly remembered dignity. Erect, she walked out.

THE VOYAGE OUT

Jeff found himself sitting next to her one night in a movie house, and when he saw that she was neat and pretty he began to watch her furtively. Though she didn't turn her head, he felt sure she was aware of him beside her. When she got up to go, he followed her out, and as she hesitated at the theatre entrance, drawing on her gloves, he began a polite, timid conversation. Then they walked along the street together.

Her name was Jessie and she worked in a millinery store and lived with her father and mother. Until one night a month later, when they were in the hall of her apartment house saying good night in the way they had so often done in the last weeks, he hadn't thought he had much chance of making love to her. They were standing close together, laughing and whispering. Then she stopped laughing and was quiet, as though the shyness hidden under her warm affectionate ways was troubling her. She put her arms tight around him, lifted up her face, held him as if she would never let him go, and let him know she was offering all her love.

"I don't want to go home. Let me go in with you and stay awhile."

"All right— if they're asleep," she whispered.

As they opened the door and tiptoed into her place, the boldness he felt in her made his heart pound. Then they heard her father cough. They stood still, frightened, her hand tightening on his arm.

"We'd better not tonight," she whispered. "They're awake. You'd better go quick."

"Tomorrow night then?"

"Maybe— we'll see," she said.

Brushing her face against his, she almost shoved him out into the hall.

As he loafed over to Eighth Avenue, he was full of elation, and he thought, "She'll do anything I want now. It came so easy, just like I wanted it to," and a longing for her began to grow in him. He could feel her warmth and hear her urgent whispering. He grinned as he loafed along, for he had thought it would take a long time and he'd have to go slow and easy. Lights in the stores, the underground subway rumble, and the noise of the cross-town buses on Twenty-Third Street seemed to be made important by the marvellous tenderness within him. He wanted suddenly to lean against a bar or sit at a counter, hear men's laughter, and feel his own triumphant importance among them, and he hurried into the restaurant where he had a cup of coffee every night after leaving her.

At this hour men from a local bakery, with the strong, sweet smell of freshly baked bread on them and their pants white with flour, came in and sat in a row at the counter. While ordering hot food they looked around to see who else was in the restaurant. There were two girls sitting at a table talking quietly. When Jeff smiled at the girls without any shyness, because a warm feeling for everyone and everything was in him, they shrugged in surprise and laughed at each other.

Sitting next to Jeff was a big, powerful, sandy-haired fellow wearing a little flour-marked cap. The others called him Mike, and Jeff had often seen him in the restaurant. Having finished his plate and wiped his mouth, he winked at Jeff and said, "Hello, kid. You around here again tonight? What's new?"

"Nothing," Jeff said. "I've just been feeling pretty good." He looked so happy as he grinned that Mike puckered his eyes and appraised him thoughtfully, and the two girls at the table were watching him, too. To seem nonchalant, Jeff whispered to Mike, as he indicated the girls with a nod of his head, "How do you like the look of the blonde doll in the green hat?"

"That one?" Mike said as he turned on his stool and looked at the girls, who were whispering with their heads close together. "That one? She's a cinch. Didn't you see the glad eye she was giving you? A soft touch. She'd give you no trouble at all."

"She don't look like that to me," Jeff said.

"If you couldn't go to town with her in two weeks, you ought to quit," Mike said. Then, as if ashamed to be arguing about women with a man who was so much younger, he added, "Anyway, she's too old for you. Lay off her."

Jeff kept shifting around on the stool, trying to catch a sudden glimpse of the girl in the green hat so he could see her as Mike had seen her, yet knowing that to him she still looked quiet and respectable. When she smiled suddenly, she seemed like any other friendly girl – a little like Jessie, even. "Maybe Mike could have looked at Jessie and known from the start it would only take a month with her," he thought. Feeling miserable, he kept staring at the girl, yearning to possess Mike's wisdom, with a fierce longing growing in him to know about every intimate moment Jessie had had with the men who had tried to make love to her. "If I had been sure of myself, I guess I could have knocked Jessie over the first night I took her out," he went on thinking. The elation he had felt after leaving Jessie seemed childish, and he ached with disappointment.

The girls, who had become embarrassed by Jeff's sullen stare, got up and left the restaurant, and when they had gone Jeff said to Mike, "I get what you mean about the doll in the green hat."

"What did she do?" Mike asked.

"Nothing, nothing. Just the way she swung her hips going out of the door," Jeff lied, and he lit a cigarette and paid his check and went out.

Jeff and his brother, who was a salesman out of work, had a small apartment on West Twenty-Second Street. As soon as Jeff got home, he realized that the sight of the food in the restaurant had made him hungry, and he went to the fridge and got a tomato, intending to cut some bread and make himself a sandwich. He was holding the tomato in his hand when there was the sound of someone rapping on the door. It was his brother's girl, Eva, tall and slim with fine brown eyes, who was only about two years older than Jeff. She often came to the apartment to see Jeff's brother. She was at ease with Jeff, and laughed a lot with him, and never minded him having a cup of coffee with them. But tonight she looked dreadfully frightened. Her eyes were red-rimmed and moist, as though she had been crying.

"Jeff, is Bill home?" she asked.

"He ought to be home any minute, Eva. I thought he was with you."

"He was, but he left me, and I thought he'd be here."

"Sit down and wait for him," Jeff said.

When she had been sitting down a little while and they were talking, Jeff found himself trying to look at her as Mike had looked at the girl in the green hat in the restaurant, looking at the way she held her head, at her legs, at her eyes – with such a strange, shrewd glance that she became uneasy and began to smooth her skirt down over her legs.

"She knew what I was thinking," Jeff thought, smiling and cynical, and he tried to say with his eyes, *I know a lot more about you than I used to know. I'll bet if I put my arms around you, you'd snuggle up against me.*

"What's the matter with you tonight?" Eva said uneasily.

Startled, Jeff said, "Nothing. Nothing is the matter with me."

"I guess I'm restless. I can't sit still. I think I'll be going," she said, and with her face flushed, she got up and went out before he could think of anything to say that might keep her there.

When she had gone, Jeff, remembering the distress in her eyes when she'd first come in, grew ashamed of the stupid, leering way he had looked at her. "I've driven her away. Thinking of Mike made me act like a fool." He hurried to the open window and he could see her pacing up and down, waiting.

He stayed at the window, watching till he saw his brother coming. Eva ran up to him, and they stopped under the light and began to talk earnestly. Then Bill took her by the arm very firmly and they started to walk toward the corner, but then they turned and came back and stood talking beneath the window.

In the murmur of their voices Jeff knew from the tone that his brother was apologetic. Then the voices rose a little and seemed to be lifted up to him, and there was a desperate pleading in the snatch of words, an eloquent sound Jeff had never heard in a girl's voice before. "It's all right. I wish you'd understand. I'm not worrying and I'll never, never hold it against you." She stopped suddenly and grabbed at Bill's arm. Then she let him go and hurried along the street, while Bill stood still, looking after her.

When Bill came in, Jeff said, "Eva was in here waiting for you."

Throwing his hat on a chair, Bill walked aimlessly toward the bedroom. "I know she was here. I ran into her outside."

"What did she want?"

"Nothing important."

"She was worked up about something, all right."

In Bill's eyes there was the same distress Jeff had seen on the face of Eva. He was accustomed to having his older brother dominate him, even bully him a little. Bill seemed years older than Jeff because his hair had got so thin. Now the worry, the wonder, and fright showing in Bill's eyes made Jeff feel helpless. "Eva thinks she's going away, but I'm not going to let her," Bill said. "I'm going to marry her even if we have to all live here together."

"Doesn't she want to marry you?"

"She keeps saying it's her fault, and I didn't intend to marry her, and now she's put me in a hole at a time when we can't do anything about it. She wants to go away for a while till everything's all right." Then Bill, looking straight ahead, said quietly, "I don't know what I'd do if anything happened to Eva."

Jeff could still see Eva clutching at his brother's arm on the street – but not in the way Jessie had clutched at his own arm – and he said hesitantly, "I've got a girl too. I wouldn't want to get in the jam you're in."

"Nobody does. There's no use talking about it," Bill said, and he went into the bedroom and Jeff knew that Bill was quietly fearing for Eva, longing to protect her. Jeff began to feel all his brother's wretchedness and grew timid. If he went back to Jessie, it might get for them like it was for Bill and Eva now.

He sat and worried about his brother for a long time. Then he knew suddenly that he was no longer even thinking of his brother; without noticing it, he had begun to dream of the way Jessie had held him and the way she was going to whisper to him tomorrow night at her place when it was very late. He could see her lifting her ardent face up to him.

Realizing that neither Mike's wisdom nor his brother's anguish could teach him anything and standing at the open window, he looked out over the lighted streets where he had walked a little while ago, looking toward Jessie's place, stirred with a longing for more and more of whatever she would be able to give him. It had started now for them and it would keep going on. And then he was filled with awe, for it seemed like the beginning of a voyage out, with not much he had learned on this night to guide him.

THE BRIDE

That last night at the hotel, Eleanor, standing in front of the bureau mirror, was smiling at herself with her warm soft eyes as she put on her black hat with the rose veil. She had been married only six days. She was such a gentle, quiet girl, with her slender ankles, her dainty hands, and the fine high bridge on her nose, that everybody who knew her thought she ought to have married a doctor or a lawyer with a good practice who could have given her some security.

Eleanor was waiting for her husband to come in and take her out to the theatre. Since she had never worn a veil with a hat before, she kept hurrying seriously from the bureau to the bathroom mirror, peering at herself and fretting and feeling quite sure that Walter's eyes would light up with helpless admiration as soon as he saw her. "Then we'll rush out to the show and rush back and get some sleep and get up early," she thought. In the morning they were going third-class on the boat to Europe. Everything was taking place so rapidly. They were alone and together, they were actually married, and there was a kind of sweet, uneasy pleasure in letting each small new experience astonish and sweep her from one day into another without letting her stop to grow timid. "I just love this little veil. It's perfect, it's stunning," she thought.

Walter, coming into the room, called out, "Are you ready, Eleanor?" As she glanced at her pretty face in the mirror, she said, "I'm all ready. I won't keep you a minute," and watched with placid assurance for him to take one long, admiring look at her before they hurried out together. He came slowly into the bathroom, hardly seeing her. There was a dreamy, pleased expression in his eyes. Walter was a lazy-moving young man of middle height whose face kept folding in warm smiles. He was carrying a newspaper opened at a particular page. In a most casual manner, to conceal his own deep satisfaction, he held out the paper and said, "Look at this, Eleanor. There's a little piece here about my winning the scholarship."

"Isn't that lovely," she said. "Is it a big piece? Let me see." She pushed her veil back from her eyes.

As he handed her the paper, he seemed rather bored, so she just glanced once at the article to see his name and the space devoted to him and then she smiled and said, "That's splendid, isn't it, dear?" Eleanor still thought they were in a hurry to go out and that he wouldn't want her to delay and read the paper. "I'm ready, darling," she said, hoping he would notice her little black veil.

But he frowned and there was a sullen expression on his face. His blue eyes got bright with bewildered indignation and he blurted out, "Do you mean to say you won't take time to read that little bit there?"

"I thought we were in a hurry, that's all," she said, but she faltered and felt disturbed beyond all reason. "I mean I thought we could read it when we came home. You told me to be sure and be ready."

"But imagine your being able to go out without reading it when you know it all means so much to me. Just imagine."

"I'll read it," she said. "Give it to me."

"Don't bother," he said, "I know you look at my work differently than I do. What's everything to me is so often nothing to you. Come on, we'll be late."

"But I said I'd read it," she cried, snatching the paper.

"Go ahead, then. Read it out of duty." He sighed, shrugged his shoulders, and said, "I can't understand you. If you're not really interested, why are you going off to Europe on a wild-goose chase? We'll have hardly any money for two, barely enough to live on. If we go broke, you'll probably want me to quit and come back and get a job."

They were in the bedroom now and she sat down by the window to try to read the piece in the paper, but the printed letters kept dancing up and down and her veil kept dropping in front of her eyes. She was hurt, yet she knew she had hurt him, too. "Why didn't I read it when he first handed it to me?" she thought. "I don't know why I didn't."

Walter was saying moodily, "Come on, let's go, Eleanor."

"If you feel the way you say, I don't want to go out with you," she said. "If you talk like that about me, I won't go to the show." But as she spoke, she pleaded with her eyes, wanting him to apologize and comfort her and say he had been wrong.

"Come on," he said irritably. "It's just a little thing. Forget it."

"You don't think it such a little thing or you wouldn't still be so nasty, so I won't go with you while you feel that way," she said resentfully.

"All right, don't," he said, blunt and angry. "I can't help it if I feel that way." He flung himself on the bed and tried to show by his inert indifference that he was a reasonable, good-tempered fellow who was interested mainly in humouring his wife. They were both silent. Then Walter began to feel miserable and more and more bewildered. In the months before the marriage, their relationship had seemed so simple, but already he had begun to feel a pulling and straining between them over very little things that was bewildering because it hurt so much. As he looked at Eleanor sitting forlornly by the window, he could not stand this separation and he felt his whole being drifting toward her. "What really matters deeply to her?" he asked himself. He thought of the hours she had listened to him talking and had seemed so animated by anything that stirred him at all. "I don't know why this has to happen," he said mildly. "I'm not going to sit here saying nothing. The whole thing is of no importance. I'm going downstairs to the lobby."

"Suit yourself," she said stubbornly.

When he had gone, she tried to behave like a sensible woman who was prepared to enjoy a quiet evening by herself. She took off her coat and hat, put on a negligée, got herself an apple, and lay down on the bed to read. The window in the room looked across at another wing of the hotel, and laughter drifting across from those lighted open windows began to make her feel restless and lonesome. Very slowly she nibbled at her apple, staring at one spot on the printed page and trying to understand how Walter could speak with so much bitterness about a simple matter of having his name mentioned in the paper, and as she frowned there grew in her a dull, heavy fear of all the trifling matters for disagreement that might arise and grow big and sharp enough to separate them. She felt even worse because her fear was so mixed up with her ache of love for him. Her mother had said, "Eleanor, you've only known the man a year. It's very silly to get married now. You'll never have anything ahead. Just because the boy has a chance to go to Europe for a year, he wants to take you with him." Within her grew an increasing dread of all the days ahead, days sure to be full of such abrupt, surprising disagreements . . . in the morning they were going far away to a strange country where she would have no friends if she should find herself alone. Even in the hotel room, where she could hear the noise of laughter from open windows, she became so afraid of being alone that she felt helpless; she began to cry.

She was still crying when Walter came in. He had made up his mind to come sauntering into the room smiling with tolerant good nature to conceal his awkwardness, so he got confused when he saw her and rushed across the room with a white, worried face, saying, "What's the matter?"

"I don't know," she said, and she kept crying.

"Can't I do anything?" he said, caressing her head.

"No, I guess I'm just lonesome, that's all. Can't I cry if I want to?"

"Why are you so lonesome?"

"I wish I were home," she said. "I don't want to go so far away."

"You're afraid of how things will turn out," he said angrily.

"Maybe I'm afraid. I don't know."

She lay with her black curled hair against the clean white pillow and heard him walking up and down, up and down, and at last she stopped crying.

"We're very silly," he said finally. "I'm ashamed. To make it worse, there was nothing to it at all. But it's my fault. Please forgive me, Eleanor."

"All right, Walter," she said willingly. "Let's forget about it. Kiss me. It's just as well we're going to bed early, when we're sailing in the morning."

He kissed her with grave tenderness, and then he said softly, almost to himself, "We ought to feel so happy tonight. Sailing in the morning, with so much to look forward to." He turned once to see her smiling at him. He smiled himself, then walked away restlessly, for he could not look contented, and he sat down by the window with his chin cupped in his hand.

His aloof dejection puzzled Eleanor, and after watching him for some time, she said, "What's the matter with you now, Walter?"

"Nothing. I feel fine."

"You can't feel fine while you look so unhappy," she said, trying to tease him. "Look at me and tell me what you're thinking about. Give me three guesses."

With a bashful grin, Walter shook his head, trying to appear offhand, then he said impetuously, "Did you read the piece in the paper, Eleanor? Why don't you look at it now and see what you think about it."

"You said you don't care what I think," she answered, still teasing him with her smile.

"You know I care, don't go on like that," he said.

She continued to shake her head firmly while he coaxed her, and as he pleaded and looked dejected, she could hardly help laughing. The more he coaxed, the more it delighted her.

"All right, then, Eleanor, don't do it," he said humbly, and at that moment, while he spoke with such humility, she realized fully how necessary her enthusiasm was to him. She realized that there could be no pleasure even in this simple matter for him unless he shared it with her, and she was filled with a warmth and joy that came from seeing how inevitably he was pulled toward her. She smiled and closed her eyes. She could hear the city street sounds far below. In the early morning they would be hurrying to the harbour, rushing to the boat. Again she grew timid. But she felt herself thrust so buoyantly into their life together that she sat bolt upright, breathless.

THE CHISELER

Old Poppa Tabb was never really cut out to be a manager for a fighter. He seemed too short and too fat, although he'd only got soft around the waist during the last year as Billy got a lot of work in the small clubs, fighting at the flyweight limit. If it hadn't been for his old man, Billy would have been a chesty little bum standing at night on street corners spitting after cops when they passed. The old man and Billy were both the same size – five foot two in their bare feet – only the old man weighed one hundred and thirty-five pounds and Billy one hundred and twelve.

Poppa Tabb had always wanted his son to amount to something and didn't like the stories he heard about his son being chased by policemen. It hurt him when Billy was sent down for three months for tripping a cop and putting the boots to him. So he thought his son might want to be a fighter and he made an arrangement with a man named Smooth Cassidy, who was very experienced with young fighters, to act as Billy's trainer and handler, and he himself held the contract as the manager. After Billy started fighting in the small clubs, Poppa Tabb bought two white sweaters with "Billy Tabb" on the back in black letters, one for himself and one for Smooth Cassidy. It was at this time that Poppa Tabb began to get a little fat around the waist. He used to sit over in the sunlight by the door of the fire hall and tell the firemen about Billy. He used to sit there and talk about "me and Billy," and have a warm glowing feeling down deep inside.

Late at night he used to wait for Billy to come home from drinking parties with fast white women. He waited, walking up and down the narrow hall of their flat, and he shook his head and imagined that Billy had gotten into an accident. When Billy came in and started to take off his shoes, Poppa Tabb, sitting opposite him, was so worried he said: "I don't want you strolling your stuff so late, Billy."

Billy looked at him. Standing up and coming closer, he said to his old man: "You tryin' to get on me?"

"No, only I know what's good for you, son."

"Yeah. Maybe I know what's good for me. Maybe I know you ain't so good for me."

"There some things you got to do, Billy."

Billy raised his fist. "You want something? You want some of this?"

"You don't go hitting me, Billy."

"Say you want some and I smack you. Or get off me."

After that, when Billy came in late Poppa Tabb just looked at his bright sharp eyes and smelled the cologne on his clothes and couldn't say anything to him. He only wished that Billy would tell him everything. He wanted to share the exciting times of his life and have the same feeling, talking to him, that he got when he held up the water pail and handed the sponge to Smooth Cassidy when he was ringside.

Billy did so well in the small clubs that bigger promoters offered him work. But they always talked business with Smooth Cassidy, and Poppa Tabb felt they were trying to leave him out. Just before Billy fought Frankie Genaro, the flyweight champion, who was willing to fight almost anyone in town because the purses for flyweights were so small, Poppa Tabb heard stories that Dick Hallam, who liked owning pieces of fighters, was getting interested in Billy and taking him out to parties. At nights now Billy hardly ever talked to his old man, but still expected him to wait on him like a servant.

Old Poppa Tabb was thinking about it the afternoon of the Genaro fight and he was so worried he went downtown looking for Billy, asking the newsboys at the corner, old friends of Billy's, if they had seen him. In the afternoon, Billy usually passed by the newsstand and talked with the boys till smaller kids came along and whispered, staring at him. Poppa Tabb found Billy in a diner looking to see if his name had gotten into the papers, thrusting big forkfuls of chocolate cake into his wide mouth. The old man looked at him and wanted to rebuke him for eating the chocolate cake but was afraid, so he said: "What's happening Billy?"

"Uh," Billy said.

The old man said carefully: "I don't like this here talk about you stepping around too much with that Hallam guy."

"You don't?" Billy said, pushing his fine brown felt hat back on his narrow brow and wrinkling his forehead. "What you going do 'bout it?"

"Well, nothing, I guess, Billy."

"You damn right," Billy said flatly. Without looking up again he went on eating cake and reading the papers intently as if his old man hadn't spoken to him at all.

The Genaro fight was an extraordinary success for Billy. Of course, he didn't win. Genaro, who was in his late thirties, went into a kind of short waltz and then clutched and held on when he was tired, and when he was fresh and strong he used a swift pecking left hand that cut the eyes. But Billy liked a man to come in close and hold on, for he put his head on Genaro's chest and flailed with both hands, and no one could hold his arms. Once he got in close, his arms worked with a beautiful tireless precision, and the crowd, liking a great body-puncher, began to roar, and Poppa Tabb put his head down and jumped around, and then he looked up at

Billy, whose eye was cut and whose lips were thick and swollen. It didn't matter whether he won the flyweight title, for soon he would be a bantamweight, and then a featherweight, the way he was growing.

Everybody was shouting when Billy left the ring, holding his bandaged hands up high over his head, and he rushed up the aisle to the dressing room, the crowd still roaring as he passed through the seats and the people who tried to touch him with their hands. His gown had fallen off his shoulders. His seconds were running on ahead shouting: "Out of the way! Out of the way!" and Billy, his face puffed, his brown body glistening under the lights, followed, looking straight ahead, his wild eyes bulging. The crowd closed in behind him at the door of the dressing room.

Poppa Tabb had a hard time getting through the crowd for he couldn't go up the aisle as fast as Billy and the seconds. He was holding his cap tightly in his hands. He had put on a coat over his white 'Billy Tabb' sweater. His thin hair was wet as he lurched forward. The neckband of his shirt stuck up from under the sweater and a yellow collar-button shone in the lamplight. "Let me in, let me in," he kept saying, almost hysterical with excitement. "It's my kid, that's my kid." The policeman at the door, who recognized him, said: "Come on in, Pop."

Billy Tabb was stretched out on the rubbing-table and his handlers were gently working over him. The room smelled of liniment. Everybody was talking. Smooth Cassidy was sitting at the end of the table, whispering with Dick Hallam, a tall thin man wearing well-pressed trousers. Old Poppa Tabb stood there blinking and then moved closer to Billy. He did not like Hallam's gold rings and his pearl-grey felt hat and his sharp nose. Old Poppa Tabb was afraid of Hallam and stood fingering the yellow collar-button.

"What's happening, Pop?" Hallam said, smiling expansively.

"Nothing," Pop said, hunching his shoulders and wishing Billy would look at him. They were working on Billy's back muscles and his face was flat against the board. His back rose and fell as he breathed deeply.

"Have a cigar, Pop!" Hallam said.

"No thanks."

"No? My man, I got some good news for you," he said, flicking the end of his nose with his forefinger,

"You got no good news for me," Poppa Tabb said, still wishing Billy would look up at him.

"Sure I do. Billy gonna be big in a few months and I'm gonna take his contract over — most of it, anyway — and have Cassidy look after him. So he won't be needing you no more."

"What you say?" Old Poppa Tabb said to Cassidy.

"It's entirely up to you, Poppa Tabb," Cassidy said, looking down at the floor.

"Yes sir, Billy made good tonight and I'm going to take a piece of him," Hallam said, glancing down at the shiny toes of his shoes. "The boy'll get on when I start looking after him. I'll get stuff for him you couldn't touch. He needs my influence. A guy like you can't expect to go on taking a big cut on Billy."

"So you going to butt in ?" Poppa Tabb said.

"Me butt in? That's ripe, seeing you never did nothing but butt in on Billy."

"I'm sticking with Billy," Poppa Tabb said. "You ain't taking no piece of him."

"Shut your face," Billy said, looking up suddenly.

"Shut your face is right," Hallam said. "You're through buttin' in."

"You don't fool me none, Hallam. You just after a cut on Billy."

"You just another old guy trying to chisel on his son," Hallam said scornfully.

Billy was sitting up listening, his hands held loosely in his lap. The room was hot and smelled of sweat. Old Poppa Tabb, turning, went to put his hand on Billy's shoulder. "Tell him to beat it, Billy," he said.

"Keep your hands off. You know you been butting in all my life."

"Sure I have, Billy. I been there 'cause I'm your pop, Billy. You know how it's always been with me. I don't take nothing from you. I don't take a red cent. I just stick with you, Billy. See? We been big together."

"You never went so big with me," Billy said.

"Ain't nothing bigger with me than you, Billy. Tell this hustler to run." Again, he reached to touch Billy's shoulder .

"You insult my friend, you got no call," Billy said. He swung a short right to his father's chin. Poppa Tabb sat down on the floor. He was ready to cry but kept on looking at Billy, who was glaring at him.

"Goddamn, he your old man," Hallam said.

"He can get out. I done with him."

"Sure you are. He'll get out."

They watched Smooth Cassidy help Poppa Tabb get up. "What you going to do about this?" Smooth Cassidy was muttering to him. "You ought to be able to do something, Poppa."

Old Poppa Tabb shook his head awkwardly. "No, there's nothing, Smooth."

"But he your boy, and it's up to you."

"Nothing's up to me."

"It all right with you, Poppa, then it all right with me," Cassidy said, stepping back.

Old Poppa Tabb, standing there, seemed to be waiting for something. His jaw fell open. He did not move.

"Well, that be that," Hallam said. He took a cigar out of his pocket, looked at it and suddenly thrust it into Poppa Tabb's open mouth. "Have a cigar," he said.

Poppa Tabb's teeth closed down on the cigar. It was sticking straight out of his mouth as he went out, without looking back. The crowd had gone and the big building was empty. It was dark down by the ring. He didn't look at anything. The unlighted cigar stuck out of his mouth as he went out the big door to the street.

LUNCH COUNTER

Ever since he had been a kid Fred Sloane had wanted to be a cook, not just any cook but a man who might some day be called a chef. For two years he had done the cooking for the O'Neils, who owned a small quick-lunch.

Mrs. O'Neil, who sometimes helped him in the kitchen, was a heavy, hard-working woman with grey hair, a very clean, sober, earnest woman, always a little afraid of her husband, whom she obeyed from a strong sense of religious duty. Mrs. O'Neil thought Fred boyish but inclined to be easy-going, a young man who grinned too knowingly and was apt to laugh recklessly when she seriously tried to advise him about a more earnest way of living. She was a good woman and because of her strong convictions would not do any work in the restaurant kitchen on Sundays. Fred liked her because she was so motherly, and he was sorry when her husband openly quarreled with her. One morning when she was very tired and had remained in bed late, her husband told Fred that she was a lazy good-for-nothing slut.

But Fred liked Jerry O'Neil, too, because he was so jovial. Jerry was a few inches over six feet, big-framed, red-faced, a bit bald. He kidded the customers at the counter, and to strangers he winked and whispered hoarsely: "You see that fellow with the cap at the end of the counter? He's sore at me because his wife's in love with me." The man wearing the cap, a steady customer, laughed heartily. Everybody laughed. Jerry shook his head as if to apologize for having so much good humour.

When they were not busy in the restaurant and Mrs. O'Neil was upstairs, Jerry talked through the wicket to Fred, who was in the kitchen. Invariably they talked about girls. Jerry had been married a long time, and though Mrs. O'Neil thought him a wild roustabout, he was far too steady and respectable to be unfaithful to her. He just enjoyed telling Fred many pointless jokes and laughing and because he was so eager, Fred used to tell him ridiculous stories about women.

A niece of Mrs. O'Neil's, very young and pretty, came to stay one night, and wanted to see them cooking in the kitchen. It was necessary for Mrs. O'Neil to help Fred during the seven-o'clock rush hour before she could have her own evening meal upstairs, and the niece was amusing herself looking around the kitchen while waiting for her aunt. Jerry O'Neil was on the other side of the wicket waiting on two customers. When Fred saw the girl, Marion, standing beside him, he smiled and adroitly flipped an omelette in the small pan. Marion was only fifteen years old but well developed, dark-haired, and round-eyed. The sweater she wore fit her tightly. Her skirt was short, the right length for a girl her age, but in a longer skirt she would have looked like a full-grown woman. She was enjoying Fred's self-assurance. Fred was glad to have her standing beside him, and out of the corner of his eye he noted her eager admiration. He tried to move with all the assurance of a first-class chef. Jerry O'Neil, pressing his wide face to the wicket called in another order. Fred, enjoying himself immensely, rubbed his hands together. He hadn't spoken to the girl. Suddenly he said: "Would you like to try and flip an omelette?"

"Show me. I don't think I could do it right," she said.

"It comes easy, just like this."

The omelette, browned on one side, turned in the air and flopped down to the pan, sizzling freshly as the blue flames licked the edge. He could hardly help laughing out loud. "Another thing," he said. "You ought to learn how to break an egg properly. Just tap it smartly once on the edge of the pan." After he had prepared another omelette, she took hold of the handle of the pan. He, too, held the handle, his hand partly covering hers, and when the omelette was done on one side, he said, "Ready," and jerked the pan upward.

The girl, her cheeks flushed from the heat of the kitchen, laughed happily. "That was good," she said. "I can do it myself now."

"You just need confidence. Cooking eggs is like boiling water. Anybody can do it."

As he stood there, hands on his hips, grinning and good-humoured, he noticed Mrs. O'Neil, who was cutting bread at the other end of the table. "If you want to get your dinner, I can look after the place now," he said.

She said sharply: "You aren't so willing other nights."

He was surprised, and then angry at the heavy, thin-lipped woman. By her sharp reply she was intimating that he wanted to be alone with her niece, that she understood his feeling when he took hold of Marion's hand to help her flip the omelette. And so she remained there, big and heavy and alert. He was especially hurt because he had been only trying to show off with the girl and had not thought of her as a woman at all; she was just a young girl who seemed to admire and like him and smiled frankly when he grinned at her. He went on working while Marion stood beside him.

Mrs. O'Neil left the kitchen. At the door she turned and said: "Come right upstairs, Marion." Fred was so angry at Mrs. O'Neil that he could not be bothered with Marion, who was examining the pots and the mixing bowls and asking questions which he answered curtly. "Mrs. O'Neil is a fool," he thought. Marion was standing beside him and he was telling her how to make a bacon and lettuce and chicken sandwich. He became more enthusiastic as Jerry O'Neil passed through the kitchen on his way upstairs. "Keep an eye on the place," he said to Fred, who went on talking with Marion till O'Neil called suddenly from the top of the stairs: "Fred, come here."

Fred opened the door and looked up the stairs. Jerry O'Neil muttered down to him: "Look here, what are you keeping the girl down there for?" His big face was red and he was angry. He had never seemed so serious. "Cut it out," he said. "Cut it out." And he added: "Tell her to come up and have dinner."

Fred returned to the kitchen. His hands were trembling. Marion was waiting for him, her hands linked behind her back, eyeing him candidly. "They're sure I'm after the kid. It's the one thing the O'Neils had ever agreed about," he thought.

"Your uncle wants you to go upstairs," he said.

"All right, he ought to call me," she said smiling. "Are you through showing me things?"

"I am."

Reluctantly, she moved to the door. She had to pass the scales used for weighing supplies. Stopping, she insisted Fred show her how to operate the scales, and then asked if he could guess her weight within three pounds.

The O'Neils had spoiled the simple pleasure he had been having with the girl, his pleasure in his own capability and, looking at her, he thought nervously of putting his arms around her and kissing her. When she was on the scales he placed his hands on her waist, his palms pressing down on the curve of her slender hips, and for no reason she put her small warm hands on his as they both bent forward to read the scales. On the nape of her neck he saw fine hair, and when she straightened, her back was arched and slender. "You're a lovely little thing," he said, almost shyly.

"I like you too, Fred," she said. By the way her hands were resting on his he knew he could kiss her. While he was having these thoughts and feeling a new need for the girl, he heard Mrs. O'Neil coming slowly downstairs. "Marion," she called, and then, "Fred."

As she went out of the kitchen Marion said, "So long, Fred," and smiled over her shoulder.

"So long, kid."

Mrs. O'Neil waited till Marion had gone upstairs, then she warned Fred: "Jerry is sore at you. He's so mad he's ready to eat you alive."

"What for?"

"You know."

"Then tell him to come down and tell me," he called after her as she climbed the stairs.

He sat on an upturned box waiting for O'Neil to come down, and knew he would not come. No one was in the restaurant; he waited, listening. He heard them talking upstairs. He would never see the girl again, he thought, and wondered why such honest, sober people as the O'Neils suddenly repelled him. Angrily he stood up, hating Mrs. O'Neil and her way of living. He hated Jerry O'Neil intensely because he had called his wife an old slut. He hated them both because they were old, and alert, and sly, and sure of what to expect from him.

THE REJECTED ONE

Karl brought her along the street early one winter evening, taking her to meet his people. As they walked in step with her elbow snug against his side, she was silent, as though feeling his uneasiness and sharing his thoughts. Karl kept glancing intently at her powdered face, at her fine shoulders, and at her thick blonde hair. He was wishing she had on a dark dress that might have looked more quietly elegant than this flowing green one. Even her hair, maybe, was too long and yellow, and her wide-brimmed black hat drooping low over her face gave her a startling full red mouth. He was trying to remember how she had looked that first time he had seen her, before he had grown to love her, but he could not remember, and as she turned and smiled at him, he seemed to feel all the warmth and roundness of her moving close to him.

"Remember that Mother's an invalid," he said cautiously. "She does funny things sometimes."

"I'll remember," she said timidly. Then she began to look puzzled, as if his seriousness had begun to frighten her.

"Anyway, you'll like my brother," he said reassuringly. "I feel sure of that."

When they went into the house, Mamie hung back a little behind Karl so that Karl's brother and his young wife could not quite see her as they came out of the sitting-room to the hall. Karl's brother was tall and slender, and had big deep-set brown eyes that kept shifting around restlessly. Karl went up to him, took his arm affectionately, and said, "This is Mamie, John. I know you'll like her. And you, too, Helen."

Then they all turned and looked at Mamie, who had been trying to keep close to Karl, but was now alone. She seemed to feel that his brother and his wife were looking at her more shrewdly than Karl had ever done. She swung her head to one side with awkward shyness. The young wife, tall and slim, with a dainty face and girlish in her simple grey dress, glanced swiftly at her husband and her face grew troubled, but she said graciously, "Won't you come in and sit down?" and she led the way into the sitting-room.

Mamie then seemed to find the words she had prepared so carefully. "I'm glad to see you, John," she said. "And you, too, Mrs. Henderson, I feel like we were old friends almost." There was so much warmth in the way she put out her large hands that Mrs. Henderson smiled good naturedly.

At the other end of the long room, a white-haired old lady was sitting in an invalid's chair. She was dozing, with her head drooping forward, but when they came toward her she opened her eyes, which were blue and soft, and so much like Karl's. "I'd like you to meet a young lady, Mother," Karl said.

"Who is it, Karl?"

"It's Mamie. I'm awfully fond of her, Mother."

"Tell her to come here and let me see her."

Karl was proud of the way Mamie stepped across the room to meet his mother: she seemed to walk across the carpet like a lovely mannequin, with a mysterious smile on her face as though she had been practising for this moment for a long time. She had never looked so elegant as she did now to Karl, so he couldn't understand why his brother turned his head away and would not look at her, or why Helen began to bite her lip and look angry.

"What's the matter, John?" he whispered.

"Nothing. Nothing at all. What do you mean, Karl?"

Mamie was saying sweetly, "Good evening, Mrs. Henderson. Karl has often talked about you to me, so of course I've been most anxious to meet you," but she spoke with an almost mechanical sedateness. Then she suddenly smiled and said simply, "What I mean, I guess, is that you're Karl's mother and that's enough for me," and she grinned broadly. For a long time old Mrs. Henderson stared at her, and then her thin lips began to tremble. Then she said bluntly like one wise woman speaking to another and sure that she will be understood, "Karl is just a boy. I suppose you know he's just a boy . . . Sit down, though, and have them get you a cup of coffee. Please don't pay any attention to me. I'm very tired." The old lady took a deep breath, closed her eyes, and would not open them again.

Mamie seemed too bewildered to move, something seemed to be holding her to the spot in spite of her resentment, while her face reddened. But she started to laugh and said, "For the love of Mike, why are we all acting so stiff?" And yet she moved over closer to Karl with a kind of independent swagger. The way old Mrs. Henderson had closed her eyes made them all feel uneasy. Young Mrs. Henderson was instantly anxious to be hospitable and friendly to Mamie. But Karl noticed that his brother was still glancing furtively at her in the way men turn on the street to watch a flashy woman who has just passed by, and he did not know whether to like this or not. "Let's sit down," he said, "and I'll tell you a story I heard today."

With a fine flow of words and many easy gestures, he told one of his favourite jokes, and for the first time they heard Mamie's loud, deep, husky laughter.

"Shall I tell one now, Karl?" she said.

"Go ahead, Mamie."

"I'd better make sure it's not the one about the salesman and the backwoods daughter," she said, her eyes crinkling slyly. But she told no story. She began to talk quite wildly, as if she had to keep on chattering or grow desperate, and all the while Karl was trying to motion to her to be quiet. When she did see him staring at her, she grew sullen and did not know what to say. For some reason that he could not figure out, Karl was ashamed. He felt Mamie's fumbling uneasiness there with his people and he remembered how proud she had been the first time she had taken him to her home. He remembered how her father, a big, rough, tousle-headed, genial man, had jumped up and put down his glasses and his paper and how he had talked to him warmly and with such respect.

"I'll go and get the coffee," young Mrs. Henderson was saying. When she had gone halfway across the room, she stopped, turned, and looked back, looking really at Karl, whom she liked and admired so much because he had such a fine instinct for pleasing people with his impulsive ways, and in this one glance backward trying to figure out what he could see in a buxom, gaudy-looking girl like Mamie, she called out, "Do you want to help me, John?" and she waited so that her husband dared not refuse to follow her.

As soon as they left, Karl said irritably to Mamie, "I never heard you talking so much. What's the matter?"

"I don't know. I just feel crazy."

"What's the matter, Mamie? Don't you think they're nice?"

"Sure I think they're nice. They're fine people, but I just feel crazy. Maybe it's the way they look at me. I don't know what I'm saying."

When John returned, he was smiling and trying to be very gay. And yet as he walked up and down making many gracious little remarks, he was obviously thinking of the conversation he had had with his wife. He was very fond of his young brother. Every time he passed him, walking up and down, he began to look at him more sympathetically. He never stopped talking to Mamie, but he was talking more quietly and easily now, and sometimes gently as if he knew all about her. The peaceful tone of his brother's voice suddenly filled Karl with hope, and he became so eager to ask him if he liked Mamie that he said, "Why don't you go and help Helen with the coffee, Mamie?"

"All right," Mamie said reluctantly. But she got up very slowly. She walked across the room with her head down, as if she could not bear to go into the kitchen and be alone with young Mrs. Henderson. Turning once, she looked back, almost pleading with Karl.

Karl said quickly to his brother, "How do you like her, John?"

"I like her all right," John said cautiously. But he would not look directly at his brother. Then he said mildly, "Do you think you're in love with her, Karl?"

"I think I am, John."

"Where did you meet her?"

"At Coney Island with a fellow from the office."

"I suppose you know all about her."

"All there is to know, John."

"I don't know what to say, Karl. She looks like a . . . She looks like a rather easy-going girl." John was hating himself for speaking this way about his brother's girl, but he was very fond of Karl and he felt he had to speak. "Like a . . . Maybe I mean not like a girl for you."

"You may have noticed the unimportant things," Karl said. Then he looked tense and said suddenly, "I'm going to marry her."

"Don't do it, Karl. It'll finish you before you start. You'll have to go her way the rest of your life. You'll see later on. Please don't."

Then Mamie and Helen returned with the coffee. But it was impossible now to make easy conversation. Maybe it was because the mother, solemn, aloof, and forbidding, was dozing in her chair and they were suddenly aware of her. They looked at each other and spoke and the sentences trailed away. Mamie had become suddenly quiet; a few fumbling words came to her, then she was still. She had begun to feel very strongly that they were reticent because they had such love for Karl, and she was trying to put it against her own love, and it gave her a wondering, shy, and lonely look. She sat very straight in her bright-green dress, with a cup of coffee in her hand and the light shining on her shoulders and fair hair under her big hat. Her mouth looked wide and red. Karl noticed the simple candor in her eyes as she looked around fearfully, and with this stillness that was in her now she looked as he had so often seen her look when he had loved her most. He felt excited. He kept glancing restlessly at his brother, wondering why he, too, did not notice Mamie now.

Then Mamie said hesitantly, "I think we'd better go."

"Maybe we'd better," Karl said.

"You say good-bye to your mother for me," she said to John.

At the door, they all shook hands. "Well, I wanted to meet you all and I met you," Mamie said.

"Good night."

"Good night. Good night, Karl," they said.

Outside Karl and Mamie were silent. They walked in step. It was fine and clear out on the street. Karl was thinking, "Why didn't they look at Mamie when she was sitting there at the end? They would have seen what she's really like." He felt angry. "That was the only time they had a chance to see what she was really like." He went on thinking how splendid she had looked, how she had suddenly been changed and had begun to look like such a fine person. "You'd think they would have noticed it," he thought. He heard Mamie asking quietly, "What do you think they thought of me?"

"I don't know yet," he said casually. But then he could not stop remembering how his brother had said so earnestly, "Please don't do it," and the voice almost coaxing, the voice gentle and full of love. "She looks like a . . ." He heard the voice still trying to finish the sentence. Now there was not fear but dreadful uneasiness and then heavy deadness within him.

"What do you think of Helen?" he asked.

"I didn't like her," Mamie said, "she's a little snip."

"She was nice to you."

"She was nice to me just as if I was her idea of a fallen woman." Then she added in a rage, "I'd like to wring her neck."

"Maybe she didn't like you either," he said angrily.

"I don't want her to."

"She's nicer than anyone you'll ever meet," he said sharply.

This sharp hostility, rising so quickly, startled them, but they welcomed it with eagerness. They wanted to hurt each other so they could pull against whatever was holding them together. They kept on hurting each other till she said quickly, "I'll not walk along here feeling you hate me. Don't come home with me. I'll go alone," and she pushed him away from her and hurried across the road.

"Let her go if she feels that way," Karl thought. So he stood and watched her cross the street, watched the swaying of her hips, and the blonde hair at her neck. He almost felt the firmness and warmth and roundness of her passing away from him.

Then he darted after her and called out, "Mamie!"

"Go away!" she called as she turned. Her face showed all that was breaking inside her. Her face, bewildered and desolate, showed how well she knew they had rejected her.

He watched her fading out of sight while he remembered all the happiness he had expected to have with her. He started to follow her slowly, feeling sure he was doing something irrevocable that could not be undone. But he only knew that he dared not let her out of his sight.

TORONTO'S CALLAGHAN
By Bernard Preston, January 18, 1936, *Saturday Night*

One of the most striking things about Morley Callaghan is that there seems at first glance nothing whatever striking about him. By this is not meant that there is nothing bombastic, or theatrical, nothing of a pose, in his makeup; naturally, one would not anticipate that, after the most cursory reading of his stories.

Even the physical aspect of him is surprisingly ordinary — though by this term is meant something far removed from what would be implied in the word "commonplace." Not tall, not large, not athletic-looking for all his record of activity in sports, though abounding in health and vigor, he would to the casual observer be easily overlooked "in a crowd," except perhaps for the fact that he is more affable than the average. And even this affability might deceive the unanalytical into mistaking it for its much more common imitation, pointless amiability.

While he talks — and for some time after he has ceased talking — one feels something distinctly vital about him. His loitering gaze seems to focus its latent keenness, though the eyes continue smiling; the full lips, very red and not invested with much impressiveness for all of the slim black moustache above them, seem to become a little more muscular; the nose suddenly appears trenchantly sensitive, an organ of true *flair*. And the absolute honesty, the sheer common-sense, and the uncompromising scrutiny of his mind radiate a clarity and warmth like that of full sunlight. But there are recesses, many of them, into which only a long-sustained gaze may penetrate, just as the strongest sunlight casts the densest shadows, though these may not be noticed at first, owing to the brilliance of what is immediately visible.

Mere things evidently do not interest him; there is a noticeable dearth of useless objects in his home. All necessary furniture is there, with comfort and convenience as prime characteristics. A few good rugs, an Italian pottery lamp that delights the eye, some very good pictures — a modern nude, a pencil sketch, himself in oils — and a marvellously intricate batik, these, with book-shelves, seem to furnish his living room more adequately than could any collection of knick-knacks, bibelots, photographs and other supposed ornaments. And this austerity, which has its own grace, is but a reflection of Mr. Callaghan's mental attitude. No clutter of trivialities there!

And what does he talk about, this laxly intent artist, this indolently active thinker? The answer is: Everything! Everything, that is, that bears relation to life. He is passionately opposed to ignorance, he must have awareness, and so spends hours daily reading newspapers from all over the world. He feels that the greatest thing in life is to get out of one's self and fraternizes with any individual who crosses his path. He loves the crowd at a prize-fight, at a foot-ball or a hockey game, at a boxing-match. He is intensely interested in politics, in the wide sense of the word, and used to speak in public, for a thirst possesses him to help toward bringing about some measure of social justice for the mass of the people.

It is this enormous catholicity in the world of ideas that makes him far more ready to be interested in others than to interest others in himself; he will discuss ships and sealing wax with equal impartiality.

He is so thoroughly detached mentally that he feels readily at home in any realm of thought or any part of the globe. Paris, for instance, he loved. He loved the Paris of streets and parks, of monuments and works of art, of history and romance; all of this he found engrossingly fascinating, and with his amazingly retentive memory recalls vividly long afterward some visual details of landscape, of Gothic architecture, of a painting, that he had at the time scarcely been aware of noting. But he loved too the human Paris, the Paris of his friends and fellow mortals; he made an acute distinction between the night-life of the Parisians' Paris and of that of the American tourist, and seemed to feel that that brilliant metropolis, emptied of his friends, might lose some of its luster for him.

Contact with alert minds is as the breath of his nostrils to him; yet such is his power of projection that he can reside for long stretches in an utterly uninspired *milieu* and yet achieve this contact at a distance. Space as well as matter seems not to exist all-importantly for him.

He is vastly amused by the tendency of the *literati* to label, to classify him. Merely because the *Nation*, on the appearance of his first novel, "Strange Fugitive," announced him as "the fashionable hard-boiled novelist of 1929" he fails to find insight in the dicta of those who still term him hard-boiled, as he has not since then written in that key, modulating indeed into that of tenderness. Others persist in thinking of him as an exponent of the underworld; and others, despite his adaptability and independent un-clannishness "wish on him" the influence of an Irish-Catholic background, of which he maintains he is quite unconscious.

Swift dashes of insight come surprisingly. A surmise, deftly sketched in a few incisive words, of what a certain individual would appear like to an-other gives a rather breath-taking portrait of both. Of a friend, a colleague in the world of letters, he will speak with illuminating analysis, with generous appreciation and with unsentimental recognition of an occasional weakness, all without at all touching on the fact of the personal relations between them; his friendship does not happen to be what he is talking about. On the other hand the infectious imagery, in which he indulges quite naturally, flashes before the listener vivid pictures worthy of a Francis Thompson. Another col-league, of whom he does not approve and for whom he cannot, one suspects, at bottom feel aught but disgust, he still contrives to discuss equably, giving full due when he can, and mitigating his final verdict with mercy. Blind Justice herself is not more impartial.

New York, restless and aimless to so many, seems to him to be aiming at some very definite goal. The coolness of the finger which he lays upon her fevered pulse enables him to diagnose without bias what may be the portent of her throbbings. He admits readily, with no sense of confession, that he likes New York better than any other place. He finds doubtless that there he can enjoy not only a freer interchange of ideas, but that ideas are much more rife and original than in most centres. The very air teems with stimulation, which to him would seem much more wholesome than the "inspiration" of some revered locality. Again, the contact of minds as preferable to interest in dead things: it is better than a city should be productive of interest rather than of sentiment. Also, since he is eminently practical, he naturally and quite defensibly responds to the tangible appreciation of the enormous reading public led by Manhattan.

His stories appear regularly in the *New Yorker, Esquire, Scribner's, Harper's Bazaar,* the *Atlantic Monthly* and others of the great American magazines. It was the house of Scribner that enthusiastically first brought him out, having noticed his work in periodicals abroad. For the remarkable fact is that his early writings, conceived in Toronto, began to appear in little magazines published in English by expatriates in Paris and elsewhere, such as *Transition, This Quarter, The Exile* (published in Rapallo by Ezra Pound), some of his fellow-contributors bearing the well-known names of James Joyce, Carl Sandburg, Ernest Hemingway, and Pound himself.

His book, "Such Is My Beloved," is to appear this spring in England, with the authoritative Methuen imprint, owing to the keen interest of the famous E.V. Lucas, chairman of the board of directors of the firm, who first read it in America and immediately determined that an English edition should appear. His latest opus, "They Shall Inherit the Earth," issued in September, is the only novel that has been vouchsafed the privilege of first seeing the light of day in the *Modern Library*, in all of the eight replete years since this well-known series was established by Random House.

His prehensile healthy curiosity will perhaps seize upon one word, dropped unconsciously, and start him on a course of inquiry leading to any topic that may develop interest. But he will just as readily drop the investigation, such is his good-nature, if it appears not to be a welcome subject to his interlocutor. With no pretense of false modesty, he will willingly talk about his own reactions, but with engaging humility he may abandon this subject — so all-engrossing to most mortals — to discuss the other fellow's.

He says that his method of creation is to think and keep thinking about his basic idea, until it takes form and becomes visible to him; whereupon he begins to feel, and continues to do so, more and more intensely, until the whole subject is so nearly complete that practically all it needs is transmission to paper. The following out of a formula, as a chemist might fill a prescription, appears grotesque to him. Art, he feels, is simplicity itself. All of which of course is all very well, if one is born an artist; and, equally of course, no method would be of the least use if one is not. Such poise invests him that he never seems bewildered and, though he prefers a non-turbulent environment when engaged at his work, he can produce it under the stress of some confusion.

"To feel so intensely that the thing writes itself," such have been more or less his words, "would seem to indicate that writing in this way is not a manifestation of the intellect. But when one remembers that all this feeling is the fruit of thought, the thought that has gradually been assembling the various factors in the story, then it will be recognized after all as an intellectual piece of work."

His elasticity of mind is such that, without losing the thread of his thought, he can temporarily put it aside, greet an interruption, deal with it with full adequacy, and then return or not to the original theme according to what seems most expedient. In the course or a particularly eloquent exposition of the difficulties of the modern writing in keeping up, or keeping on, he will stop for a few good-night words with his little son Michael, a lad with the eyes of a Raphael cherub, and eyelashes that would turn a Hollywood beauty green with envy. Comes the final embrace with the little feet pattering off to bed, while the author will resume telling of the incessant necessity of constantly bettering one's own record, if popularity is to be retained.

These then are some of the qualities that compose that remarkable person, Morley Callaghan, born in Toronto only thirty-one years ago. An extraordinary lack of self-consciousness, with its corresponding humility, an intransigeant honesty, a sense of justice; together with a ready friendliness toward the whole world, an imagination never allowed to run riot, a fine sense of proportion; also an abhorrence of the personally spectacular, a taste very nearly impeccable without the least fastidiousness, and a good-humour frequently expressed by a short laugh almost like the chuckle of a school boy. He reconciles a profound knowledge of the world and a mature youthfulness with an apparently artless ingenuousness and young wisdom, and exercises keen critical ability with seeming carelessness. In other words, he embodies equipoise, balance, sanity.

Altogether a distinguished figure, albeit quite unpreoccupied with dignity or distinction (which are the greater for it), an already brilliant son of Canada destined for still far greater brilliance, of whom the Dominion may boast with all due pride.

Questions for Discussion and Essays

1. In his Editor's Notes to Volume One of Morley Callaghan's *Complete Stories*, Barry Callaghan remarks that Morley Callaghan "has that delicacy so much more important than verbal delicacy, the delicacy of accumulated perceptions, which brings the sense in the end to a grasp of recognition." What is the difference between "verbal delicacy" and "accumulated perceptions?" How are accumulated perceptions used in a story such as "The Shining Red Apple"? How do these perceptions accumulate and lead to the resolution of the action of the story's final paragraph?

2. Morley Callaghan (and contemporaries such as Ernest Hemingway) came of age in the first half of the 20th century with a style devoid of metaphor and often described as "plain talk." And yet, despite their plain-speaking style, Callaghan's stories are meticulously constructed. What devices does Callaghan employ to create a sense of "plain speak"?

3. Does this "plain talk" style evoke any broad social or literary attitudes of the era in which the stories are written? If so, what keeps them relevant today?

4. In many of these stories, ordinary objects desired, purchased, or owned by the characters carry intense symbolic meaning. What is the role of the stockings in "Silk Stockings," and "Timothy Harshaw's Flute"? Do these objects perform the same role as the pony in "The White Pony"?

5. Morley Callaghan told an interviewer that it was never his practice to "carry out a theme." Rather, he said, it was his job to "catch the tempo, the stream, the feel, the way people live and

think in their time, quite aside from any intellectual matters." This set him apart from ideological writers, the Marxists or orthodox Catholics, of the thirties, because in his stories the meaning was not imposed from without; the action, limited and small as it might seem, was the meaning. Discuss.

6. For Callaghan, the real tragedy of the Depression years lay not in economic collapse itself, but the number of lives undone and left uncompleted, and the number of stories told that were cynical, stories of inevitable defeat. Callaghan said that he was listening all through these years for "a lustier crowing," for signs of passion, for signs of yearning and a hope that could not be broken, even by poverty. Discuss.

7. Each of Callaghan's stories moves toward an epiphany – that is, a moment when not only the reader comes to a sudden realization of the deep moral meaning of what has happened to the characters, but the characters themselves come to such an awareness. Only a writer of deep religious sensibility could believe in the possibility of such epiphanies. Discuss Callaghan as a religious writer.

8. One of Callaghan's characters says, "There is a unity of life on earth, and it will reveal itself if I stop passing judgment on other people, and forget about myself, and let myself look at the world with whatever goodness there is in me." Is it true that most of Callaghan's characters are disinterestedly and even compassionately presented, regardless of class or criminality? Does Callaghan live up to his claim that as a storyteller he wanted to be as compassionate and as anonymous as the stone carvers of the cathedral at Chartres?

Selected Books by Morley Callaghan

Callaghan, Morley. *The Complete Stories, Volumes 1-4.*
   Toronto: Exile Editions, 2003.

Callaghan, Morley. *It's Never Over.*
   Toronto: Exile Editions, 2004.

Callaghan, Morley. *A Literary Life. Reflections and Reminiscences,
   1928 - 1990* (non fiction).
   Toronto: Exile Editions, 2008.

Callaghan, Morley. *The New Yorker Stories.*
   Toronto: Exile Editions Classics Series, 2008.

Callaghan, Morley. *Strange Fugitive.*
   Toronto: Exile Editions, 2004.

Callaghan, Morley. *That Summer in Paris.*
   Toronto: Exile Editions Classics Series, 2006.

Callaghan, Morley. *A Time for Judas.*
   Toronto: Exile Editions, 2005.

Callaghan, Morley. *The Vow.*
   Toronto: Exile Editions, 2005.

Related Reading

Anderson, Sherwood. *Winesburg, Ohio*. Introduced by Malcolm
 Cowley. New Edition.
 New York: Milestone Editions, 1960.

Callaghan, Morley. *A Literary Life. Reflections and Reminiscences,
 1928 - 1990* (non fiction).
 Toronto: Exile Editions, 2008.

Conron, Brandon. *Morley Callaghan*.
 New York: Twayne, 1966.

Dreiser, Theodore. *Sister Carrie*.
 New York: W.W. Norton, 2005.

Farrell, James T. *Studs Lonigan (A Trilogy)*. Pete Hamill (editor).
 New York: Library of America, 1998.

Flaubert, Gustave. *Madame Bovary*. Margaret Cohen (editor).
 New York: Norton Critical Editions, 1998.

Hemingway, Ernest. *The Complete Short Stories*.
 New York: Charles Scribner's Sons, 1998.

de Maupassant, Guy. *The Complete Short Stories of Guy de
 Maupassant, 1955*. Artine Artinian (editor).
 London: Penguin, 1995.

Joyce, James. *The Dubliners*.
 London: Penguin, 1999.

Websites of Interest

http://www.athabascau.ca/writers/mcallaghan.html

http://www.cbc.ca/lifeandtimes/callaghan.htm

http://www.editoreric.com/greatlit/authors/Callaghan.html

http://www.todayinliterature.com/biography/morley.callaghan.asp

http://www.thecanadianencyclopedia.com/index.cfm?PgNm=TCE
&Params=A1ARTA0001178

http://www.britannica.com/eb/article-9018691/Morley-Callaghan

http://www.track0.com/ogwc/authors/callaghan_m.html

http://www.biographybase.com/biography/Callaghan_Morley.html

This book is entirely printed on FSC certified paper.